For unto you is born this day in the city of
David a savior, which is Christ the Lord.
—Luke 2:11

Chapter One

"No, no, no. If she doesn't see that he's using her, she doesn't deserve him." Isabelle Grant wadded up a piece of paper and threw it at the television.

"Mom, it's a movie." Lizzie stood at the door, long, dark hair pulled back in a ponytail. When she wore it like that, she still looked like a little girl and Isabelle didn't feel thirty-three.

But her daughter was twelve and getting older every day. Lately it seemed as if they had changed roles. Lizzie was forgetting that Isabelle was the mom and she was the daughter. Isabelle clicked off the television and stretched. She had to be at the Hash-it-Out Diner, Gibson, Missouri's one and only restaurant, in thirty minutes, for the evening shift. And Lizzie, as on so many evenings, would be home alone. At least they had a great neighbor in the duplex next door. Mrs. Jackson kept an eye on things.

"I know it's a movie, but the characters should still make wise choices."

"Yes, wise choices. I remember that lecture."

"Cheeky kid." Isabelle hugged the child, who had sat down next to her on the sofa. "I love you."

"You know, Mom, I think you might be addicted to the Hallmark Channel."

"That was Lifetime."

"Whatever. They're all the same."

"Are not."

"Sappy movies and docudramas."

"Okay, so what would you prefer me to watch?" Isabelle drew one leg up and turned to look at the child who was blossoming into a beautiful young woman. She wanted to stop the clock, to keep it from happening.

For a long minute, Isabelle felt alone, really alone. She ached deep inside, reminded that someday Lizzie would spread her wings and fly away to her own life, her own dreams, her own happy endings.

Isabelle prayed there really would be happy endings for her daughter.

"Mom, I don't care what you watch. I just wish your life was about more than those movies. You should go out on a date."

"I don't need to date." Because she had loved the best man in the world, and he'd been taken from her.

"You need to do more than work and raise me."

Isabelle looked hard at her daughter. "When did you grow up?"

"Last year. I'm preteen now, remember?"

"Yeah, I remember. And you'll be thirteen in March."

"And I really, really want to go to the dance camp in Tulsa. I asked Jolynn, and she said I could help her

clean house this winter. She'll pay me. I can save money, and you won't have to work another job."

Big sigh. Isabelle *so* did not have the money for dance camp. But maybe, if she could do more book-keeping at home in her spare time, or work an extra day at Ed's Garage on the outskirts of Gibson, where she was a mechanic. But if the extra money went to camp, how would she take care of Christmas, just a month away?

"Mom, don't look so worried. I know we might not be able to afford it."

"But I *want* to afford it, Liz. I really want to give you everything."

"You're always telling me that we don't get everything we want in life."

Isabelle closed her eyes, remembering that lecture, the one she gave when she didn't have the money to give her daughter everything she wanted to give her. Moms didn't get everything they wanted, either. Sometimes dreams were expensive.

"I love you, Lizzie." Isabelle hugged her daughter close. "And now I have to hurry or I'll be late. Jolynn will have my hide."

"No, she won't."

The doorbell rang. The two looked at each other. Isabelle peeked and couldn't see who was on the front stoop. "Are you expecting someone?"

"Nope."

Isabelle glanced out the window. A truck was parked in the drive. A new truck. "Oh, goodie, I think we've won a new truck. That has to be it."

She opened the door, leaving the chain in place. Gibson, Missouri, wasn't dangerous, but that didn't mean she had to be careless. A man stood in front of the door. A man in a military uniform. His presence took Isabelle back, but in her memories it wasn't a soldier on her step—it was a police officer. Thirteen years, and she still remembered that night. She could still feel the rip of pain that tore through her heart as the officer told her that her husband had been killed in a car accident.

She could still remember holding her belly, where the unborn Lizzie was safe, not knowing that their world was falling apart. She remembered telling the trooper she didn't have family to call. The officer had called Jolynn, because he'd known her from church.

The soldier on her front step cleared his throat and smiled. Man, he was gorgeous. His dark hair was shaved short, and his skin was tan from too much time in the sun. When a smile broke across his face, dimples split his cheeks and white teeth flashed.

"Surprise!"

She blinked, because, yes, she was surprised, but she didn't have a clue what he meant by that. Maybe she'd won a soldier, not a truck? Behind her, Lizzie gasped, and then her footsteps retreated down the hall to the bedroom.

"Surprise?" Isabelle didn't want to sound like an idiot, but she was clueless. Had she met him before? Had she entered a sweepstakes, and the prize was a soldier for Christmas?

She unhooked the chain and opened the door the rest of the way.

"I brought you something." He smiled again and held out a bag. "Sand from one of the holiest sites in the world."

He handed her the bag with a ribbon tied around the top. She blinked a few times and tried to think of something to say. Asking him who he was would have been a start.

"Isabelle, are you okay?"

No, of course she wasn't okay. She had to go to work. Tonight after work she and Lizzie were going to cut down a tree for Christmas. A stranger had just handed her a bag of sand, and he knew her name.

How could this be right?

She looked at the name on his uniform. Daniels. The name sounded familiar but she didn't know anyone in the military.

"I'm sorry, do I know you?" When she asked the question, he frowned.

"Well, I guess you don't, not really. But after a year of writing letters, I guess I thought…"

"Whoa, wait a second. Writing letters?" Isabelle wanted to sit down. She glanced at her watch. She now had fifteen minutes until she had to be at work. She remembered a letter, last year, a Christmas letter. She hadn't written it, though.

"Letters, Isabelle, and packages. I just processed out of the military, and thought I'd stop and say hello."

"Letters?"

His hazel-green eyes were staring at her like she was a crazy woman. "The letters you wrote to me…or maybe didn't write."

"Lizzie, front and center." Isabelle thought about

letting him in, but she wasn't going to let him into her home. She didn't know if he was really a soldier. He might be the crazy one, not her.

Lizzie slunk down the hall. Her face was pale, her brown eyes huge. And she had that look on her face, the one that made her look more like her father and less like Isabelle. The guilty-but-sheepish look.

"Mom, I can explain."

"Please do."

"I should come back." Chad Daniels spoke, backing off the stoop.

"No!" Isabelle and Lizzie said at the same time. The soldier looked like retreat might be his best option. Though he didn't look like a guy who retreated. He looked like a hero to Isabelle. And she couldn't go there.

Isabelle took a deep breath to compose herself. It didn't work. "Wait. We'll figure this out."

"I'm the one who was writing to you." Lizzie turned from pale to pink. "Our class sent packages to Iraq, and when we got the letters back, I got a letter from you. And you sounded like a really great person. You sounded…"

The Christmas letter. Realization dawned slowly, and Isabelle wanted to groan as the pieces of the puzzle came together.

She waited for her daughter to finish, but Lizzie didn't. Instead her eyes overflowed with tears, and she bit down on her bottom lip. "I'm really sorry."

"How did I sound? I mean, other than sounding like a great person." Chad stood at ease on their sidewalk, tall and with shoulders so broad they stretched the

desert-sand camouflage of his uniform tight across his chest. His gaze, serious but gentle, was fixed on Lizzie.

Isabelle leaned against the door frame and waited for her daughter to answer. Lizzie glanced from the soldier to Isabelle and then back to the ground, her teeth biting into her bottom lip. Finally she looked up. Her brown eyes overflowed with tears, and she sniffled.

"Like you needed a friend." Lizzie looked from him to Isabelle and that's when she knew what her daughter had done and why.

"Oh, Liz, you shouldn't have." Isabelle covered her eyes with her hands and wished the ground would swallow her. "I have to go to work."

"I guess I have to leave."

"There aren't a lot of places to go," Lizzie offered, a tentative smile back on her face. "I mean, you could go to Springfield, but you weren't looking for a city, you were looking for a real town, a community. There's a bed-and-breakfast here, just down the road. It opened up last year."

"Lizzie, stop." Isabelle stared at the soldier—a man, not a boy.

"I think I'll drive around Gibson and decide what to do." He smiled again, and he didn't look lost or confused. Those emotions were Isabelle's, obviously. "Lizzie, you're a great kid. I really enjoyed our letters. I'm a little embarrassed now, but that's okay. You did a sweet thing, wanting two people to be a little less lonely."

He saluted and walked away, long strides, strong and in control. Isabelle's insides were shaking, and she didn't know what to do next.

But she had to go to work. As the truck drove down the street, she turned to face her daughter. "I can't believe you did that. I'm a grown woman, Lizzie. I don't need to have my twelve-year-old daughter arranging my love life."

The truck turned the corner, and she wondered if she had seen the last of Chad Daniels. Not that it mattered.

But if it didn't matter, then why in the world did it make her feel sad? Only one reason made sense. She felt sad for him. It was nearly Christmas, and he'd come to town thinking he'd find a friend. Instead he found that he'd been tricked. By her daughter.

"You have to apologize." Isabelle grabbed her purse and gave her daughter a look that Lizzie knew well. "You can't play with a man's emotions that way. It isn't fair."

Life isn't fair. One of the many lectures she'd given in the past. Sometimes life even hurts. Officer Chad Daniels probably already knew that.

Chad drove to the parking lot of a deserted old gas station. The concrete was cracked, and weeds had grown up and then died in the cold of winter. Cold. He liked that feeling. He liked the damp, brisk air that smelled like wood smoke from fireplaces and drying grasses, maybe a little fertilizer from a nearby farm.

But now what? He'd been writing to a kid for nearly a year, believing she was a woman. An adult woman. His face warmed, and there wasn't anyone to witness his embarrassment. He could only imagine what the guys in his unit would say. They would have teased the old guy who had gotten duped by a kid. His face burned a little hotter. He rolled the window down all the way.

Those letters had taken him into the life of a woman he'd never met. Isabelle—dark hair, dark eyes and unspoken dreams that she had never shared. Her husband had died before the birth of their first child, Lizzie.

The real author of the letters, that child.

He smiled a little, because the kid had spunk. He should have seen it in the letters, the sometimes childish scrawl in her handwriting. He should have known it was a girl, not a woman.

But it was Isabelle's story, her life, that had brought him here. The stories of a town that took care of its own had drawn him to Gibson. A town that helped a widow, raised money when someone was sick or provided when a family lost their home to fire—those were the things he wanted.

He had been in a foreign country fighting for towns like Gibson to stay safe, to remain in their peaceful cocoons where Christmas was still about a Nativity in the park and "Silent Night" was sung during a community gathering. He had been fighting to give that freedom to towns in a foreign country, to people who had dreams of their own.

Lizzie might have written the letters, but the town of Gibson was real. He had fallen in love with a community he'd never known before her letters. He wanted to meet Jolynn and eat pie at the Hash-it-Out Diner. He wanted to watch the lights come on during the annual Christmas Lighting Festival, held the first Sunday in the month of December.

Somewhere deep inside he admitted that he wanted to get to know Isabelle Grant, because her smile had been the first thing he thought of when he touched American soil two months earlier.

A car pulled up behind him. Lights flashed blue, and the door opened. A young cop, tall and cautious, got out of the car. Chad reached into his back pocket for his license.

He was ready for the officer, but the guy didn't take the paperwork. "I don't need those. I saw you sitting here and thought you might need help. There's a garage down the street."

Ed's Garage where Isabelle worked three days a week, changing oil and fixing small mechanical problems.

Chad read the guy's name tag and smiled, because he felt like he knew the people in this town, thanks to Isa… No, thanks to Lizzie's letters.

"Thank you, Officer Blackhorse. I'm fine—just needed a minute to think. Is there a hotel in this town?"

A hotel? Why would he do that? He could drive on to Florida, where his parents had moved last year. He could visit a buddy in Colorado. He was forty, retired, and he could go anywhere. Why would he stay here, in a town where he didn't know a soul? Okay, he knew two souls, but didn't really know them.

"You okay?" Officer Blackhorse leaned closer, peering into the truck, surveying the contents. He looked relaxed, but Chad noticed that his right hand remained on his weapon.

"I'm fine." He pulled off his hat and tossed it onto the seat next to him. He might as well tell Jay, the guy that had recently gotten married to the waitress, Lacey Gould. Chad actually had pictures of the officer's wedding. "I got played by a kid. I've been getting letters from a woman, but they were letters from her

daughter. I think it might have been an attempt at matchmaking."

"Lizzie Grant?" Jay Blackhorse grinned.

"That's the one. I wanted to meet the woman behind the letters."

"Cute kid, but a little feisty. Isabelle has her hands full. That girl is her life, though."

"So I should leave town?" Chad looked down the main street of Gibson. A truck with a lift bucket had stopped by a light pole, and a city worker was stretching Christmas lights across the street. It had been three years since he'd had a real Christmas.

"I wouldn't leave if I wanted to stay." Officer Blackhorse rubbed the back of his neck and followed Chad's glance to the street ahead of them, the stores, the cars lined up in parking spaces. "If you're looking for a temporary residence, there's a bed-and-breakfast, the Pine Tree Inn. If you want permanent, I have a house for rent in the country. And there are places to buy."

"Why don't you direct me to that bed-and-breakfast, and then maybe we can get together and talk about the house in the country."

He was retired. He wanted to have some land, a few horses, some cattle. He'd been dreaming this dream for three years.

"Directions. I can do that." Jay pulled a pen and a small tablet out of his pocket. "Here's the address and directions to the Pine Tree. And my phone number if you need anything."

"Thank you, Officer Blackhorse. I'll be seeing you around."

"I'm sure you will. Oh, and if you need a meal, the Hash-it-Out Diner and the convenience store down on the corner of Main and Highway 15 are about the only places in town."

Chad nodded and started his truck. Jay Blackhorse backed away from the truck, still grinning. Chad waved as he pulled out of the parking lot.

He was staying in Gibson. He couldn't explain why. Maybe because he didn't have another plan. Maybe because of dark brown eyes and a winter sky that looked heavy with snow. And he hadn't seen snow in a long time.

Chapter Two

Isabelle tied the apron around her waist and took another sip of the cola she'd poured when she arrived for work. Jolynn, owner of the Hash-it-Out, slipped behind her and into the waitress station, mumbling about the waitress who hadn't refilled the ketchup bottles before she took off on some hot date.

"She's young." Isabelle defended the waitress, feeling lighthearted in spite of her daughter's huge mistake coming to light. A year of letters, starting last Christmas. Only a few, Lizzie had assured her. Because they had written to soldiers for a school project the previous year, and Chad had written back to her, sounding a little sad, a little lonely.

"What's up with you today?" Jolynn lifted the big ketchup container and started to pour ketchup through a plastic funnel into the squeeze bottles that they kept on the tables.

"Nothing." How did she admit that a man had shown up on her doorstep?

"Oh, honey, I've seen that scrunch between your brows before. That isn't a sign of nothing. That's a sign of…" Jolynn grinned. "That's a sign that your daughter has been up to something. I love that girl. What did she do this time?"

Isabelle covered her face with her hands and shook her head, trying not to laugh…and not to cry. "Am I really so pathetic, Jolynn?"

"Well, honey, not in my book. But I imagine if you tell me the story, it'll make sense from the perspective of a twelve-year-old."

"She's been writing to a soldier and signing my name."

"Now, isn't that sweet. That isn't so bad, is it?"

"He showed up today."

Jolynn's mouth opened, as if she had planned to say "Oh," but nothing came out. Her eyes widened, and then her chest heaved a little. Laughter bubbled up from the older woman, and tears trickled down her cheeks. She set the ketchup bottle down and wiped her eyes with the corner of her apron.

"Oh, Isabelle, that's about the funniest thing yet. I do love that girl."

"You would take her side. Jolynn, I can't let this go. I mean, I know she did it because she loves me and she thought it would be romantic." And in a way, it was. If she hadn't been embarrassed—no, mortified—she might have been touched. "She needs to be grounded or something."

"I'm sure she's sorry."

"Not as sorry as she should be."

The cowbell over the door clanged. Isabelle slipped an order pad in the pocket of her apron and grabbed a glass of water.

"Take care of the customer. I'll figure this out," Jolynn said as she went back to pouring ketchup.

"Come up with something good. I'm at the end of my rope with that girl."

"I'll come up with something good. And I'll keep her busy working, and that'll keep her out of trouble."

Jolynn winked as Isabelle turned and walked out of the waitress station.

It really did take a village to raise a child. Isabelle smiled at the thought, because the town of Gibson had loved them and cared for them since Lizzie's birth. The child had more aunts, uncles and grandparents than any other child Isabelle knew.

She headed for the table by the window. The customer looked up, and Isabelle stopped. She didn't groan, but she wanted to. Chad smiled and dipped his head in greeting. That smile was dangerous. He shouldn't be allowed to do that in public, not in the presence of unsuspecting women.

"Isabelle." He put the menu down. "What do you recommend?"

Leaving town was an option, but she didn't say it, just smiled at the thought. "Depends on what you like. I love Jolynn's cashew chicken. Other people like chicken-fried steak."

"I'll have the cashew chicken. No cashews. I'm allergic."

"Got it. One chicken and rice."

"I'm really sorry about today. I guess I shouldn't have just shown up like that, knocking on your door without warning."

"I'm not sure how you could have made the situation any better. And I'm the one who has to apologize, for what Lizzie did."

"Don't. She was great, trying to help two people, you and me. Sweet girl."

"Yes, sweet and sneaky."

"You said she…" He stopped and shook his head. "Nope, that was her, telling me she's a beautiful dancer."

It was funny, Isabelle couldn't deny that, and she even laughed. Her daughter didn't mind tooting her own horn. "Yes, she's a dancer, and really quite talented. She wants to…"

"Wants to what?"

"Nothing. I'll put this order in." She turned away from him, because he wasn't a friend or someone she knew. He was a stranger who had shown up on her doorstep. A stranger who knew things about her life. How much did he know?

Heat crawled up her cheeks again.

"Hey, before you leave, I wanted to tell you, she didn't mean to hurt either of us."

Isabelle turned. Lizzie had hurt him. She hadn't thought about it like that, about him being hurt by the letters. What had he expected to find when he came to Gibson?

"No, she didn't mean to hurt anyone."

"Good, I'm glad you agree. Oh, I was told that the owner of this café, Jolynn, has a B and B with a vacant room."

Isabelle started to laugh. Of course the inn had vacancies—it was in Gibson. Who came here? Sometimes families in town had company and no extra beds. That was about it.

"Yes, she has vacancies. I'll send her out."

Jolynn was waiting inside the waitress station. As Isabelle rounded the corner and slipped past her, the owner of the Hash-it-Out was leaning against the counter, fanning herself with an order pad. "Wow."

"Stop." Isabelle poured a cup of coffee for their customer.

"Honey, you don't need to punish that girl of yours. You need to give her a medal for bringing that man to town. If you aren't interested, I can tell you someone will be kissing him under the mistletoe before the month is over."

"He wants to talk to you." Isabelle lifted the order. "I'm taking this to the kitchen."

As she walked away, she was imagining him under the mistletoe, and it wasn't a stranger in his arms. She shook off the vision. She really needed to stop watching those movies.

Jolynn was a motherly woman with her hair dyed light blond, and coral lipstick that framed her smile, making it bigger and brighter. Chad could see why everyone in the community loved her, including Lizzie. Because it was Lizzie who had written the glowing things about her mother's employer.

Jolynn helped them through rough times, brought them to her home for Christmas and never let them eat Thanksgiving dinner alone. Instead she had a big dinner

at the restaurant for people who didn't have a family to gather with.

One more thing he had loved about Gibson, as he had compared it to his childhood and the many times it had been just his mom, his siblings and himself, eating dinner and waiting for his dad to call.

When Chad had picked the military as a career, he had made a decision not to marry. He had kept his heart intact by never dating a woman more than a few times, never letting himself really get to know her.

The letters from Lizzie, letters about Isabelle and her daughter, had been the longest relationship of his life.

He hadn't really thought about it as a relationship before, but now he realized that he knew more about her than he knew about anyone else, except maybe the guys in his unit. As an officer, he had known a lot about his men, their families, the problems they faced. No one had really known him. Until he had shared his dreams with a girl who wasn't Isabelle Grant.

He had shared that he hadn't really known his dad.

Isabelle had shared that Lizzie had never known her father. She had encouraged him to talk to his dad. He was forty, and a twelve-year-old posing as her mother had done that for him, because she would have loved the chance to know her dad, to talk to him just once.

He leaned back in his chair, still holding his coffee cup, not really thinking about where he was, or who was watching.

"Hey, soldier, how's that coffee?" Jolynn sat down across from him like she'd known him his entire life.

"It's great coffee, thank you."

"Well, that's good to know. I like a good cup of coffee, myself. Now, how can I help you?"

"I'm looking for a place to stay, maybe a month or so. I'm not sure yet…"

"Not sure where you're going to land?"

"Exactly. But I do like the idea of spending Christmas in Gibson."

"It's a good place to spend the holidays. Or even to stay for a lifetime." She winked and poured more coffee from the pot she had carried out with her. "Don't get in a big hurry. Just pray and let the Good Lord guide you."

"I'm not in a hurry." He leaned back in his chair. "I guess, for the first time in years, I've got nowhere to go."

"Sometimes a person needs that." She smiled, her eyes so kind he felt like he could tell her anything. For a guy who never told anyone anything, that was a strange moment.

"Yeah, it isn't so bad."

"I have a nice suite that I think you'd be comfortable in. Before you leave, I'll give my husband a call and have him meet you over there so he can let you in."

"Does it have a kitchen?"

"Oh, no, but I provide breakfast here at the restaurant every morning, and you can help yourself to whatever is in the fridge. I don't mind if you cook something up, either. As long as you clean it up when you're done."

Who did that? Chad now knew the answer: Jolynn. She opened her home and obviously her heart up to strangers. And hopefully no one would ever take advantage of that fact.

The kitchen door opened, and Isabelle walked

through the swinging double doors. She paused, holding a plate that steamed. Her dark hair was held back in a clip, and the black apron was hitched low on her hips.

Isabelle, a foster child who had married a boy she met in a group home and then was widowed before her daughter's birth. That was one of the things he knew about her. But it wasn't something she'd told him. Now everything that he knew felt like whispered secrets that she hadn't shared. The pink in her cheeks was understandable.

He felt that thud of letdown, because he had really thought they would be friends, that they were already well on their way to friendship. And now she was a stranger.

"Here's your supper." She held the plate and carried a pitcher of water. "Did you get things worked out with Jolynn?"

Her employer stood, and as Isabelle put the plate down in front of him, Jolynn slid an arm around her shoulders and gave her a light squeeze. Chad wondered how long it took a person to become a part of this community. He had a feeling it took about five minutes.

"We worked it out," Jolynn answered. "Oh, and I forgot to invite Chad to the Christmas program at the firehouse this Sunday night."

"The first Sunday of the month," Chad finished for her. He had purposely shown up in town this week because he didn't want to miss that program.

"Yes, of course you know that." Jolynn filled his cup again. "And church is at eleven on Sunday morning."

She hurried away, leaving him alone with Isabelle, who shifted from foot to foot, her gaze not connecting with his.

"I'll have you over for dinner some night," she offered. "We should do something to make this up to you."

"You don't have to. It was all an innocent mistake. One Christmas letter and a chain of events. No big deal. It did bring me here, and this is a little bit of what I've been looking for." Maybe his entire life.

"I know, but I do feel bad."

He didn't want her to feel bad. He wanted her to be a friend. "Okay, if it'll make you feel better. I heard you make a great roast."

"Lizzie." She sighed, but then she nodded. "Okay, roast it is."

Chad watched her walk away and then dug into the chicken and rice, as she'd called his cashew chicken without the cashews. And he thought about Sunday and how wrong it was for him to pursue this relationship. Worse, he kept thinking that he didn't want to wait until Sunday to see her again.

Chapter Three

Isabelle was off work on Fridays. And today, because of morning snow, Lizzie was out of school. It didn't take much snow for Gibson to call off classes. She and Lizzie had spent the morning doing laundry and cleaning house. Then they'd made chocolate-chip cookies.

Now it was late afternoon and they were going to watch movies, with the house still smelling like cookies and the spicy scent of the candle Lizzie had lit. Isabelle curled up on the couch and waited for Lizzie to change into sweatpants.

Isabelle wanted something to take her mind off the man that had invaded her life, eating at the restaurant every day for the last four days—since the day he'd arrived in Gibson.

"I start my job at Jolynn's on Monday." Lizzie plopped onto the couch next to Isabelle. "Chad's living there, she said."

"Yes, he moved in right after he left here."

"Don't you think he's cute for an old guy?"

Isabelle flipped through the channels, trying to find something romantic and sweet but safe for a twelve-year-old. "I don't think he's old."

"He's forty, and he's never been married."

"Lizzie, you shouldn't know these things about his life. We haven't really discussed this, but it was wrong of you to write those letters. Really wrong." Isabelle's stomach turned a little at the thought. "It's wrong, and you could have gotten him in trouble."

Lizzie bit down on her bottom lip, and her eyes narrowed with worry. She was a sensitive little soul. "I just wanted you to meet him. He was so nice when I wrote to him, and I told him about you and our life here."

"And then *I* started writing to him." Isabelle wanted to be amused, but the sick feeling in the pit of her stomach won out over amusement. "It was a lie, and you used that poor man."

"He was lonely, too. You're both lonely."

"I'm not lonely. I have you." Isabelle picked a movie, a teen romance that she'd seen more than once. "I have an entire town of people who love me."

And she disliked every activity between now and the new year because she would spend them all alone, or as a single mom. There'd been a few times in the past friends had tried to fix her up on blind dates, and a few offers from single men at church. She'd turned them all down because she was too exhausted with work and being a mom to date. But Lizzie didn't need to know that.

"You don't have someone. Everyone should have someone. I'm not going to be here forever, you know."

Twelve. Isabelle had to remind herself that her daughter was twelve. "No, you won't be. But even when you're gone, I'll be fine."

"What if I go to camp for a month?" Lizzie's mouth was a straight line of seriousness.

"I'll be fine. I'll work. I'll have my friends."

Lizzie nodded in the direction of the television and the movie just coming on. "You'll have movies and a box of tissues."

Isabelle grabbed the remote off the coffee table, bumping her tea glass and nearly tipping it. She turned off the movie that started with a pretty college student tripping all over herself when a cute guy said hello.

"Lizzie, no more. We're not going to keep talking about this. I'm the adult. You're twelve. I really do know a little about life, and about what makes me happy. You make me happy. Your attempts at matchmaking—not such a happy moment for me. Especially when your matchmaking lures some poor guy to a town where he knows no one. As a matter of fact, I want one last letter from you to him. A letter of apology."

Lizzie's bottom lip was between her teeth, and she nodded. "I can do that. And you're right, I shouldn't have interfered. I just wanted…"

A dad. Isabelle knew what her daughter wanted. And if either of them said it, they would both cry. Lizzie wanted to know the man that she could only identify through old photographs. Dale, a young man with dark hair and a small scar on his cheek. He'd been Isabelle's knight, a tall, skinny kid who had worked hard and always managed to smile.

He'd had a habit of finding the good in every situation. A lot like his daughter, Lizzie.

"When are we going to get our tree?" Lizzie crawled up next to Isabelle and snuggled close. "It isn't rainy or snowy today."

"Maybe tomorrow morning. You know I don't like to drive on these roads."

"Okay." Lizzie flipped the television back on and changed from the movie to a cartoon. But even the cartoon squirrel had a boyfriend.

The low rumble of an engine grabbed Isabelle's attention. She leaned back on the sofa and peeked outside. Chad Daniels, in her driveway. Isabelle shot her daughter a look—in time to catch Lizzie sucking in a smile that had nearly escaped.

"I hold you personally responsible for this, my little chick." Isabelle kissed her daughter's forehead. "Not only have you complicated my life, but you've ruined sappy movies for me."

"That's because the real thing is better." Lizzie did smile then. "You've been hiding in those movies for years, Mom. It's time you experienced real life, and maybe some real romance."

"I have a life." She had already had marriage. Now she had a daughter, two jobs and hands that were dry from dishes and too much cleaning. She also had a gray hair. She'd found it last week when she'd given herself a trim.

But Chad was knocking on the door, and she didn't have time to continue the discussion with her obviously unrepentant daughter. Or the thoughts about the life she was convincing herself she possessed.

* * *

This was crazy. Chad stood looking at the green door with the Christmas wreath hung over the window, and he knew he'd lost it. He was forty, his palms were sweating and he had a chain saw in the back of his truck.

Not because he had gone crazy, but because he had experienced a sudden burst of Christmas cheer.

"Hi." Isabelle stood in the doorway.

It took him a minute to recover, because she was beautiful in sweats and a T-shirt. And she was standing in front of him, her feet bare and dark eyes serious. He had been in town for a few days now, and he knew more about her than any woman he'd ever known. She liked hot chocolate with peppermint sticks, and she cried when the choir sang "Amazing Grace." He had learned that from Jolynn's husband, Larry, who thought of Isabelle as a daughter, the child he'd never had.

"Hey?" Lizzie peeked over her mom's shoulder, her smile huge. "What are you doing here?"

"I'm, uh…" Floundering. He sighed, because this wasn't him, this person who had lost control. He had retired as a lieutenant colonel in the army. He had served during war. He knew how to command troops and bring them home safely.

He didn't know how to deal with this woman or the child standing behind her.

"Here for cookies?" Lizzie offered.

"No. Actually, I came by because I knew you were planning to get a Christmas tree, and I happen to have an extra one in my truck."

"You have an extra tree?" Isabelle said in a way that made it incredulous, not a question.

"I went out to look at the Berman farm today, and Larry and Jolynn asked if I would cut them down a tree while I was there. I went ahead and cut down two."

Her dark brows shifted up, and she laughed. "What if we already have one?"

"I'd give it to Jolynn's neighbor. Mrs. Sparks hasn't decided yet if she wants a tree." He winked, because he enjoyed watching her get flustered.

"She always waits until the week before Christmas." Isabelle motioned him inside, rubbing her arms after she pushed the door closed. "Are you staying in Gibson?"

Did she care? He wondered if he wanted her to care.

"I'm thinking about it. I went out to look at the Berman farm. It's a shame they have to sell."

"They're moving to Springfield. They have kids up there, and it's getting hard for the two of them to care for that much land."

"It would be a lot of work to keep up with a place that size." One hundred acres and a two-story farmhouse with four bedrooms. He had made an offer. "About the tree?"

"We can have it. Right, Mom?" Lizzie was hopping a little, peering over Isabelle's shoulder. "We were going to have to get one anyway."

Chad turned his attention back to Isabelle, and he could tell she was struggling with the decision. Her teeth worried her bottom lip, and she was staring past him, where he knew there was nothing to look at. Finally she nodded.

"Okay, we'll take the tree. Will it fit in here, or do we need to trim it?"

"It'll fit." He pulled his gloves out of his pocket. "I'll bring it in."

"We can have hot cocoa and cookies while we decorate. Mom makes the best homemade cookies." Lizzie's smile split across her face, infectious and sweet.

"Does she?" He smiled at Isabelle, but she didn't smile back. "I'm really just here to drop off the tree."

"You have to stay and help us decorate. What fun is cutting down the tree if you don't get to at least put the lights on it?" Lizzie glanced from him to her mother.

"Lizzie, I'm sure Chad has somewhere else…"

He shook his head. "No, not really."

Decorating the tree hadn't been part of his plan, but now that he was in her living room, close to her, he wasn't ready to leave.

"Okay." She gave Lizzie a look that he was sure she hadn't planned for him to notice. "I'll go find the decorations, if you want to bring in the tree."

"I'll put cookies on a platter and find the star. I think I put it in the hall closet last year." Lizzie slid out of the room on her stockinged feet. What kid wouldn't want to slide on hardwood floors?

"Good idea." Isabelle's gaze lingered on the door even after Lizzie was gone.

"She's a great kid. I hope you've forgiven her."

Isabelle turned. "Of course I have. She owes you an apology, though. I explained to her how wrong it was for her to deceive you that way, and the troubles it could have caused. She's young."

"I know she is. But it wasn't such a bad thing. I'm here, and Gibson is the town I thought it would be. It isn't a complete loss."

He rubbed a hand over his face and groaned, because that hadn't come out the way he'd planned. The guys in his unit had been right about one thing: he was inept when it came to women.

Isabelle touched his arm, the gesture surprising him. There was a lot about her that surprised him. Like the fact that she'd remained single. "At least you got the town you were looking for."

Her hand moved back to her side, and she walked away, leaving him in the living room, alone. He glanced around, taking it in, this real picture of who she was and the life she'd lived.

One thing he knew from this room was that she loved her daughter. There were school photographs of Lizzie, one for every year of school. Eight pictures, starting with a five-year-old girl, brown hair in pigtails. On the bookcase was a photo of a young couple holding hands. She wore a wedding dress and had stars in her eyes.

He turned away from the photograph, because it was too personal. And it connected dots, the things Lizzie had shared in letters signed with Isabelle's name.

He walked out the door, thankful for the cold air of early December. He pulled on his gloves and lowered the tailgate of his truck to pull out the tree. Six months ago, this town and this house had come to life, painted by the words written by a twelve-year-old girl. Now he was here, and he didn't know why he had stayed.

But then again, maybe he did. Because the real

Isabelle, the woman standing at the window watching him, was more captivating than the letters written by her daughter had made her out to be.

And Gibson felt more like home than any place he'd ever been. No matter how he'd gotten here, it felt like the place where he could live the rest of his life.

Isabelle opened the door as Chad pulled the tree toward the house. She stepped back, laughing when the monstrous cedar got stuck in the doorway. Lizzie cheered him on, telling him to turn it a little to the right. He grunted and tried her suggestion.

"Do you think it might be too big?" Isabelle asked as he gave it a heave and pulled it into the living room. She closed the door behind her and pointed to the corner where she'd put down the tree skirt and the stand.

"I measured it. It's six feet tall."

"But it will be taller once we get it in the stand."

"And put the star on top." Lizzie stood, hovering at the edge of the action.

"I think it'll be fine." He smiled over his shoulder, and Isabelle knew that he didn't believe it. He knew it wasn't going to fit.

"While you get it set up, I'll untangle the lights."

"Untangle?" He pulled the tree to an upright position, lifted and set it in the stand that Lizzie was holding.

Isabelle held up the strands of lights, but kept a cautious eye on her daughter. Lizzie was screwing the bolts into the tree trunk while he kept it in position. What would Lizzie do if he left? If he decided not to buy that farm or stay in Gibson?

"We should have put the lights back on the holder they came off." Isabelle looped the lights back through an opening in the cord. "We never do, though."

"That is a mess. If you wait, I can…"

"I can do it." Isabelle kept working. "And the tree is too tall."

"It'll be fine. Look at how full it is." He motioned with his hand, like she'd won the prize on a game show.

"It's perfect." Lizzie looked up from her position on the floor, screwing in the last bolt of the tree stand. She stood, backing up to look at the tree. "There's a little bare spot, but we can turn it and it'll be great."

She turned the tree and stepped back by Isabelle.

"Yes, it's perfect. Here are the lights. I'll start the cocoa."

Because she couldn't do this with Chad Daniels. She couldn't stand next to him, stringing lights on a tree, not with the photograph of Dale on the bookcase reminding her of the two Christmases they had shared—and all of the ones without him, when it had been just her and Lizzie.

Chad smiled at her like he understood. Chad in a red flannel shirt and jeans, his work boots laced up, covered in red-clay mud.

Mud. She looked at her hardwood floors, the dried mud showing the path he'd taken. "Your boots."

He looked down and groaned. "I'm sorry. Get me a broom, and I'll clean it up."

"No, don't worry about it. I'll sweep it up. You two put the lights on the tree."

He grinned, flashing those white teeth. And his eyes

sparkled with humor. "You want out of untangling this mess."

"Exactly." And she escaped, because that's what it was really all about.

From the kitchen she could hear their laughter, her daughter's and Chad's. He was giving her directions, his voice low and gentle. Lizzie chattered about the decorations they used. The ones they'd bought and the ones they'd made.

Isabelle stirred water into cocoa, added sugar and a dash of cinnamon and then mixed it into the milk on the stove. She poured in a little vanilla and kept stirring. The aroma of the cocoa lifted as it began to steam. And Isabelle tried not to think about her daughter decorating the tree with Chad, and not her.

It had always been just the two of them, Isabelle and Lizzie. This had been what they did together for years. Decorating the tree had been their moment, their time and their memories.

This year Christmas included a stranger, a man brought into their lives through letters her daughter had written. Isabelle turned off the stove and walked back into the living room. She stood at the door and watched as Chad took the star from Lizzie and placed it on the top of the tree. That had always been Isabelle's job. Things changed. Life changed. She knew that and sometimes even told herself to prepare for it. This hadn't been one of the scenarios she had played out in her mind—this man, Christmas. Her star.

He was standing precariously on the stool, and

Isabelle had to smile, because he was cute and Lizzie was hovering like she might catch him if the stool tipped.

"Don't fall," Isabelle warned.

He wobbled a little and grabbed, steadying himself with one hand on the wall. "Thanks. I'll be careful."

He put the star in place, plugged it into the lights and then nodded at Lizzie. She plugged in the cord, and the tree lit up, just lights and a star, no decorations yet. But it was pretty in the dark, shadowy room with the sky outside hovering between gray and white as dusk fell, no sun to set because clouds had kept it hidden all day.

"Help us hang the decorations, Mom." Lizzie held out the round bulb that Isabelle hung every year. The one she'd bought the year she turned eighteen, when she and Dale had married.

They had married the week they left the group home they'd spent their seventeenth year living in. Before that they'd both been bounced around from foster home to foster home. Through those tumultuous teen years they'd kept in touch, keeping one another's spirits lifted through letters and phone calls.

She'd been the daughter of a drug addict who overdosed when she was ten. He'd been the son of abusive parents who could never really get their lives together enough to be parents.

And now, here Isabelle was, a single mom. But she had survived, and Lizzie was having the childhood that Isabelle and Dale had planned for their daughter.

Chad took the decoration that Lizzie held and handed it to Isabelle. "Come on. I cut it down, you have to decorate. That's your job."

She smiled a little, and it wasn't easy, because her eyes were flooding with unshed tears, and his eyes were soft with compassion because he knew her stories. She didn't know how much he knew, but she was positive Lizzie's letters had shared too much.

But not the things Lizzie didn't know. There were things she would never know. Isabelle met his warm gaze and saw something in the dark depths of his eyes. He had stories, too. She wondered if he would ever tell them to her. Or why a man followed letters to Missouri.

"Thank you." Isabelle didn't look at the decoration in her hand. She knew that it had a picture of the Nativity on one side and a verse on the other. And in her heart she knew that Chad Daniels wasn't going to share his stories.

"Put it here, Mom. In the middle." Lizzie pointed to what she thought was the perfect place, and Isabelle nodded and hooked it in place. The pungent odor of cedar filled the house, mixing with the leftover scent of fresh-baked cookies, making it smell like Christmas.

"We need Christmas music." Isabelle's throat was tight with emotion, and she turned away from the curious gaze of the stranger who had invaded their lives.

"And we need hot cocoa so we can finish." Lizzie hung a red ornament and then a gold one. "I'll fill our cups, and you finish this."

Isabelle flipped on the television and turned to the satellite station with Christmas carols. "Okay, but be careful."

"I'll be careful, Mom. I won't burn myself."

Chad laughed a little. "It's a never-ending job, isn't it?"

"What?" Isabelle handed him a small box of ornaments.

"Being a parent."

"Yes, it's never-ending. But I wouldn't trade it for anything. You've never…" She didn't know anything about him.

"No, never been married, never had a child. I was a military brat, and I made the military my life. I guess it was a comfortable place for me. It's what I know."

"That's honorable." And she now had pieces of his life, making it a little more even, since he had most of hers in letters she hadn't written.

He shrugged and hung an ornament up high. She stood back, away from him. "I loved my career. Now it's time to find something else to…"

She wondered if he had planned on saying *love.*

He smiled as he stepped back from the tree. "Something else to do. I've always wanted to have a farm."

"Really?" She had wanted that, too, but she felt old sharing that dream with him.

"Yep. My grandfather was a farmer in Nebraska. We didn't get to see him often enough, but I always loved the time we spent there."

She'd never really known her grandparents, either. But for different reasons. Her family was dysfunctional as far back as she could remember. She'd learned stability from the foster family that had kept her, the last foster home she'd been in. They kept her until she turned seventeen, and then they'd left the state, and she had hoped they would take her.

They had written, but she hadn't seen them again.

"Lizzie says you're a mechanic." He said it like he couldn't believe it.

"Trade school. We had to pick something, so we both…" She glanced at the picture of herself and Dale. "We picked the automobile field. I picked mechanics. He picked body repair. We were going to start a business."

"I'm sorry." His hand rested on her arm, and she couldn't move away from the tenderness of his touch. It was warm, that hand on her arm, and strong.

She hadn't expected that touch to mean something. She let out a deep sigh and brushed away tears.

"It's okay. It was a long time ago." And she had Lizzie.

Speaking of Lizzie, she was singing along to the radio, a song about Christmas cookies. It was George Strait, and they both loved George.

"We should get busy, before she thinks we've been…" Chad laughed. "Sorry, that wasn't what I meant. But I do think she means for us to decorate the tree."

"She does." Isabelle pulled out a small box of ornaments she and Lizzie had made with baked dough and acrylic paints.

"I like this one." He held up an ornament shaped like the manger. "We decorated our tree with paper snowflakes last year. Let me tell you, I'm not good with paper and scissors."

"What's it like over there?" She wondered if he had shared the stories in the letters he'd written, the letters she hadn't read or even seen.

"It was good, watching the progress. Sometimes it was a heavy load, keeping the people in my unit together, keeping their spirits up."

"Have you always gone to church?"

"Didn't you read…" He laughed. "No, you didn't read the letters. Lizzie, could you tell your mom when I became a Christian?"

"He was thirty-five and in Afghanistan with a crazy Christian kid in his unit who wouldn't stop praying. And they were always safe with that kid praying." Lizzie walked into the room carrying a tray with three steaming mugs of cocoa.

"There you go." Chad smiled and shook his head. "That kid is now twenty-five and a youth minister in Texas. I guess he was never a kid."

"Cocoa and cookies." Lizzie put the tray down on the table. "Let's take a break."

As if she was the adult chaperoning two kids. Isabelle looked up, meeting the soft, warm gaze of the man that her daughter had brought into her life. This wasn't a movie, or a book. It wasn't a fairy tale.

It wasn't a first date.

And what she felt, fluttering inside her heart, getting trapped in her lungs, was all about this moment in time, about his smile, the way his hand had felt on her arm.

It was about her own loneliness, something she'd been trying to deny for a few years. It had sneaked up on her, waiting until she was done with diapers, sleepless nights and those first few years of school to rear its ugly head. But she kept busy, with work, with Lizzie, and she convinced herself she didn't have time for relationships.

"About church on Sunday." Chad sat down with a mug of cocoa and a cookie. Lizzie choked on her cocoa,

and Isabelle looked up, afraid of what this meant, and afraid to let her daughter believe that this could be everything she wanted it to be.

Or maybe afraid to let herself believe.

"Yes, church."

"Since I've crashed your tree-decorating party, what if I just meet the two of you at the town lighting ceremony Sunday night?"

"Yes, that would be good. Everyone will be there." Isabelle hated that she sounded like a chicken. But meeting at the lighting ceremony was safe. It was public. It wasn't about two people brought together by one little matchmaker.

Chapter Four

Sunday evening Chad walked down the sidewalk from Jolynn's to the metal building that served as the fire station for the Gibson all-volunteer fire department. He wasn't the only one walking. There were groups of people walking together, and families with children. Every parking space was filled, including the parking lot of the Hash-it-Out.

The fire station was next to the small city park, and he could see the lights that had been strung up. Tonight was the night those lights would be turned on for the first time. And houses that had been decorated would be lit up as well. He had helped Larry decorate the Pine Tree Inn that morning.

He had asked why they did it this way, the entire town lit up for Christmas on the same night. Larry said it was about community. It was about Christmas being about Christ's birth and not watering it down by lighting up two months early, so that by Christmas, no one noticed

anymore. And the central part of the lighting ceremony was the Nativity in the park.

This ceremony was a community worship service, not just a ceremony about lights or displays.

The weather had cooperated by making it feel like Christmas. The air was brisk, a little damp, and wood smoke billowed from the chimney pipe that stuck out of the fire-station roof. Chad stopped to watch the crowds, his gaze landing on a familiar figure, a tall brunette with a nearly teenaged replica at her side. They were both wearing plaid jackets and caps. The door to the building opened, letting out a swath of light and the sound of laughter and conversation. They moved through the door with a group of people that he recognized from church.

He walked through the door alone, not a part of any group or church. But he'd been to church that morning, to the little community church attended by half the population of Gibson. He had sat behind Isabelle and Lizzie, watching as mother and daughter, heads bent, discussed something in soft whispers. He had listened as the pastor spoke about God's gift of love in the form of His son, Jesus.

Chad had sat in that church, feeling as if he'd been attending there all his life, thanks to Lizzie's detailed descriptions in her letters.

And now he was at the lighting ceremony. He stepped into the metal building that wasn't quite warm, even with the fire in the woodstove. People stood in groups, dressed for the weather in heavy coats and gloves. He greeted a few of the people he'd met around town, and then he searched the crowd.

"She's over here, soldier." Jolynn hooked her arm through his. "I'm so glad you stayed in town. This is a good place to put down roots."

"I haven't quite decided if I'm staying."

Jolynn patted his arm, and he noticed that she had painted her nails red and green for the occasion. "Where else would you go?"

"My parents live in Florida."

"That's a good place, too. But Gibson, well, I moved here about thirty years ago, and I couldn't imagine living anywhere else."

Neither could he, but he wasn't ready to tell that to the owner of the Hash-it-Out. He smiled, and she nodded toward a group standing in the corner of the building, near fire equipment and extra hoses for the truck that had been backed out of the building for the night.

"Our church choir is over here. Come on—we need a good tenor, and if I heard right at church this morning, you're just the guy."

"Well, I don't think I'd say I'm a 'good tenor,' but if you're not picky, I can fill the part."

"You'll do just fine."

As he walked up to the group, Isabelle smiled a shy smile, and the impact of the gesture hit him square in the gut. Or maybe near his heart. A smile had never made him feel like that, and he definitely didn't consider himself a romantic kind of guy.

So why had he come to Gibson, looking for Isabelle Grant, a woman who watched romantic movies on TV and cried when she read books with happy endings?

"Here's the guy we've been looking for." Larry,

Jolynn's husband, held out a song sheet. "They assigned us to sing 'Beautiful Star of Bethlehem.' Do you know that one?"

"I think so." Chad read over the lyrics, and somehow, as the group moved, he got pushed to stand next to Isabelle.

"My daughter started a conspiracy," she whispered, smiling a little, laughter twinkling in brown eyes. He knew she was talking about the way the two of them were being pushed together. "They mean well."

"I know they do. Do you think I mind standing next to you?" In the closeness, his shoulder brushed hers.

"Do you mind the gossip of a small town?" She kept her gaze straight ahead.

"Not at all."

Another church group moved to the center of the room, and the crowd grew quiet as they started singing "Silent Night." Chad stood at Isabelle's side. Children, not interested in singing, were sitting on the floor or playing in groups. A baby cried.

He remembered a year ago, singing carols with the men in his unit around the tiny tree they'd decorated. And he remembered a letter from a young girl in Gibson, telling him about her Christmas, her mother and this celebration.

Six weeks later he'd received that first letter signed with Isabelle's signature.

The song ended, and another church group moved forward.

Standing next to him, the real Isabelle, not the letter, not the image he'd created, shivered as the door opened and another group of people entered. He shrugged out of his coat.

"Here, take this." He draped it over her shoulders.

"I'm fine. It was just the draft when the door opened. And you'll need it when we go outside."

"I have on a heavy sweater." He held the coat out so that she could slip her arms in. "There you go. And to be honest, I enjoy the cold air."

Her gaze softened. "What's it like, coming back?"

"It's an adjustment."

"You came here, instead of going home to spend Christmas with family." There were questions in that statement, and he realized she didn't know him. Of course she didn't.

"If I go home for Christmas, it would be to Florida, where my parents live now. They have an active social calendar. They usually don't put up a tree, and Christmas dinner is at a restaurant. I came here because of the letters. I wanted this for Christmas." He nodded at the crowd gathered inside the fire station.

"I understand. I couldn't imagine being anywhere else."

Jolynn motioned them forward. "Time to sing."

The group of about twenty moved to the center of the room. And Chad stood next to Isabelle, a part of the community, a part of the lives of these people. He'd always had the military community, and they were tight, but this was a place a guy could call home. Military life meant moving in and out of lives and communities.

At the front of the group candles were lit, and next to him, Isabelle sang in a soft soprano. The room was dark, and they stood in the center of the glow of candle-light, a song about a star of hope and promise echoing

in the metal building. He could hear the people around them singing along.

Chad never wanted to leave Gibson, that feeling. His arm brushed Isabelle's. Their fingers touched, and he wondered if she would ever agree to more than a moment in public with him. Would she ever sit across from him in a restaurant, or tell him the stories that Lizzie had already shared?

At times he thought she might, but then she retreated into that shell, a place where he thought she probably kept memories of her husband and the shattered dreams the two had shared.

The song ended, and the candles went out. The group turned and left the center of the room as the overhead fluorescent lights came on. Their song had been the last, and the garage doors at the end of the building went up.

"What now?"

Isabelle smiled up at him. "The lights come on in the park and down Main Street, and then Santa rides in on the fire truck."

"Fire truck?"

"Well, of course, you can't expect him to drive a sleigh in Missouri." Her smile sparkled in her eyes, and someone pushed his arm on the other side.

"Hey, guess who's under the mistletoe." Jolynn pointed up.

Chad's gaze went up, to the twig of mistletoe hanging from the door frame. Isabelle groaned a little, her face upturned as she looked from the mistletoe to him.

"You have to kiss her." Lizzie was at his side, her grin mischievous and a little guilty.

"I don't think..." Isabelle bit down on her bottom lip.

"I don't think we can ignore mistletoe." Chad brushed her cheek with his hand, and her eyes closed.

Isabelle held her breath, waiting, unsure. She hadn't been kissed in so long, except by Lizzie. And tucking a child in at night wasn't the same as a breathless moment with a man whose eyes were warm and whose smile touched somewhere deep inside.

A hand on her cheek drew her back to the present, to the cool night air, the scent of cedar from the nearby Christmas tree, and Chad.

She opened her eyes as he lowered his head, and when his lips touched her cheek, she thought he sighed. The moment was sweet, and his hand was on her neck. When she thought the kiss would end with that innocent gesture, he moved from her cheek, barely grazing her lips. And then he pulled away, his gaze holding hers. Her breath caught in her chest, getting tangled with emotions she hadn't expected. It hurt, like thawing out after being in the cold too long.

But cold was good, because it brought numbness. This feeling hurt deep inside, where she hadn't hurt in so long.

A tear slid down her cheek, and she wiped it away with her gloved hand. The next one he caught with his finger, and then he kissed her again.

"I'm sorry," he whispered in her ear as he moved away. "But I'm not sorry for being here with you."

Christmas music on a radio, tinny-sounding but cheerful, broke the moment, and everyone moved away, forgetting them, forgetting the kiss. Everyone but Isa-

belle. She couldn't forget that moment when his lips had touched hers, or how his hand had been so gentle on her cheek.

The fire truck came up the street, blaring Christmas music, red lights flashing into the dark night, reflecting off the windows of nearby businesses. Santa was on the truck, tossing candy to the children and wishing them all the blessings of Christmas. And he had his dogs with him. Isabelle smiled, because everyone loved Santa and his dogs.

"He looks like Santa," Chad whispered. "What's up with the dogs?"

"We all call him Santa, and those are his dogs. Dasher, Dancer, Comet, Cupid, Donner, Blitzen, Vixen and Rudolph."

"This is something our letter writer forgot to mention."

"She probably didn't think about it. He's been a fixture here for years. He's a retired minister, and he runs the local food bank. He might call himself Santa, but he knows the reason for Christmas is Jesus. He even made the Nativity for the park."

"I love it here."

"It's a great place to live. I'm always thankful that this is the dot we picked on the map, the place we decided to call home."

His fingers slid through hers, and he pulled her a little closer. Maybe because it was Christmas, or maybe because of the mistletoe, but Isabelle didn't pull away. Instead, she stood with him, watching as children grabbed up the candy that had been thrown from the truck.

After Santa's fire truck faded into the night, Isabelle turned toward the park, Chad's hand still holding hers tight. The crowd of people engulfed them, everyone moving together.

"Where are we going?" Chad leaned to whisper in her ear.

"Time for the lights to come on in the park."

People started to sing "Joy to the World." Isabelle blinked a few times, because this was the part where she always cried. This was like the happy ending of a movie, when it all worked out the way it was supposed to.

"Are you crying?"

She nodded but didn't look up, couldn't look at the man standing next to her. "I always cry at happy endings."

He gave her hand a light squeeze, and at that moment the lights came on. The entire town glowed with brilliant reds, greens and twinkling clear lights. The Nativity lit up with soft lights that were hidden behind the carved figures of Bethlehem.

And it was Christmas. Isabelle felt it in her heart, felt that moment when it all made sense, this season of rushing, buying, spending, sometimes worrying. This was what it was all about, this baby, this savior, and not the gifts or the rush, or the worry.

For this moment, everyone remembered. And she wished they could always remember and not lose sight of what was real, what really meant something.

"Come on, guys, time to go back inside for cookies and something warm to drink. And door prizes. This year I'm going to win." Lizzie grabbed Isabelle's other

hand, the one that Chad wasn't holding. And that left Isabelle between the two, between her daughter and the man her daughter's letters had brought into their lives.

"What do we do now?" Chad whispered in her ear as they walked through the big garage door, back into the fire station. The building was concrete floors and metal siding. Fluorescent lights hung from chains, and wood smoke scented the air.

"We go inside for door prizes."

"That isn't what I meant. What do we do now, after 'Operation Mistletoe'?"

Isabelle shrugged, hoping to pretend they didn't have to do anything. As if that kiss wouldn't be the talk of the diner tomorrow. She wanted to tell him it was Christmas and they were both lonely. That kiss hadn't been about them. It had been about the moment, the music, the lights and a sprig of green mistletoe.

"Why do we have to do anything?" She didn't look at him. They were threading their way through the crowds of people. "It's Christmas, and we're not the first ones to get caught under the mistletoe."

"I see."

She glanced up this time, because his voice was quiet.

"It's Christmas," she repeated and then searched for Lizzie, who had run off after they entered the building. "I hope she wins something. She deserves to win something."

"She's a great kid."

Isabelle laughed a little. "I'm glad you can see that, after what she did."

"She had good intentions."

"Yes, she meant well. But she shouldn't have."

"Isabelle, it's okay. She brought me here. I've found a place in the country that I can call home. The only thing I regret is that the friend I thought I'd find isn't really the friend I thought I'd been writing to for the last year. But that's okay. Maybe we can work on that part."

"I think we can be friends."

"Nothing more?" He had led her to the one quiet place in the building, and his eyes, dark and warm, studied her face with an intentness that made her look away.

Isabelle shivered and pulled his coat, a coat that had his scent, his warmth, closer around her. "Chad, I don't know about that. I mean, my life is complicated. I have to concentrate on raising Lizzie, on working two jobs. Dating has been at the bottom of my list of priorities for a long time. I'm not even sure if I remember how."

"Maybe I can help you remember." He winked and still held on to her hand. "We could find that mistletoe again."

She smiled a little and moved her hand from his. "I think for now we should avoid the mistletoe."

Lizzie's shout that she'd won ended the conversation. Isabelle turned as her daughter ran toward them, holding leather work gloves and a can of coffee.

"I won!"

"You certainly did win." Isabelle hugged her daughter. "That's just what you've always wanted, right?"

Lizzie's eyes sparkled with laughter and youth. "You can have the gloves." She handed them to Chad and then held the coffee out to Isabelle. "And you get this.

"Merry Christmas." Lizzie stood on tiptoes, twelve-

years-old and full of life. She gave Chad a loose hug. Isabelle liked that his face turned a little red and he wasn't quite sure what to do.

"We should go now." Isabelle shrugged out of his jacket and handed it back to him. "Thank you."

He took the coat. "You're welcome. And I'll see you tomorrow, right, Lizzie?"

"Yes, my first day of work. I'll be at the Pine Tree Inn after school."

Isabelle had forgotten, and now the reminder settled like a cold lump. Her daughter was determined to earn money for the dance camp that Isabelle couldn't afford. At twelve, she was determined and unwilling to give up on her dreams.

Isabelle prayed she wouldn't be let down.

Chapter Five

Chad parked his truck just as Lizzie Grant skipped up the sidewalk of Jolynn's inn. It was thanks to her that he was here. He finally had a hometown. He had signed the paperwork on the farm today, and in two months it would be his.

Lizzie, in jeans and with her plaid coat buttoned to the neck, stopped on the porch and waved, waiting for him. He got out of the truck, slipping his keys into his pocket as he walked. Lizzie, full of youthful exuberance, came down off the porch, her smile wide. She looked like her mother, tall and slim, with her dark hair long and pulled back in a ponytail. Her mom wore hers loose.

The main difference between mother and daughter was the expression in their eyes. Lizzie's eyes were full of hope, full of laughter. Isabelle had lived a lot of life, and it hadn't always been easy.

"Hey, are you ready for your first day of work?"

Lizzie nodded and stepped next to him as he went up the stairs. "All ready."

"Your mom says you're saving for dance camp? It must be pretty expensive."

"It is, really expensive." She bit down on her lip and kept her gaze down. Like her mother. And he knew she wasn't telling the whole truth.

"Something tells me this is about more than camp." He opened the door and motioned her through, into the large Victorian with the polished oak woodwork and heavy antique furniture. The back sitting room, next to the dining room, was his favorite. The furniture in that room was leather and comfortable. Larry said that room was the one place in this house where he could really relax. The rest was Jolynn's doing. She liked frilly.

Lizzie obviously liked frilly, too. She went into the first room, the drawing room with furniture that was as comfortable as a wooden bench. The floors were covered with floral area rugs, and sheer white drapes covered the windows.

"What's up, Lizzie?"

She walked around the room, her back to him, touching the books on the shelves and then pausing at the porcelain figurines that lined the mantel. She finally sat on the edge of the floral sofa, her legs crossed at the ankles and her hands clasped in her lap.

"I want to buy my mom a Christmas present." She looked up, her brown eyes liquid and her smile a little tremulous. And he didn't know what to do. He'd dealt with tears before, with young soldiers who were homesick and wanted to go home, with new parents that

hadn't seen their babies. But this, a twelve-year-old girl wanting to buy her mom a Christmas present, this was a new experience.

He cleared his throat and stood in front of her, trying hard to think of the right thing to say for this moment. She watched him, waiting, as if he was supposed to have the answers.

"What about camp? Your mom thinks you're saving money to go. And won't you be disappointed if you don't get to go?"

"I can always go to camp next year." She glanced away, but not before he saw that look, the one that said she probably wouldn't get to go. "But my mom, she's given me everything. She's given up a lot that she wanted, so I could have what I want. She works two jobs so that I can take dance lessons. She's done all of that to give me my dreams, and I want to do this for her."

He sat down in the chair next to the sofa. "What is it she wants, Lizzie?"

"She's always talked about playing the guitar. She grew up in foster homes and never got to take lessons. It's the one thing she's always wanted. And working here, I can get her a guitar. There's one at the Main Street Flea Market that she's talked about. But when I tell her to get it, she shrugs it off and says it isn't important."

"How about if I help?" He leaned forward a little, and she did a sharp double take, meeting his gaze.

"I don't know." She held her bottom lip in her teeth, and he could see that she was considering it.

"It must be a pretty expensive guitar. I could match whatever you earn."

"And then maybe we could buy the guitar and the case." Brown eyes lit up, and she was smiling again. "I think she'd really like that. She shouldn't have to give up all of her dreams."

"No, she shouldn't." He couldn't explain the way his chest tightened because he wanted Isabelle to have everything, too. He wanted her to have dreams come true and happy endings that made her cry.

But how would she feel if she knew that Lizzie was giving up camp so she could have something she wanted? Proud of Lizzie. That's how he would feel, how he already felt.

"Hey, are you going to come to my Christmas recital for ballet?" Lizzie had switched subjects, and he had to let go of his thoughts to catch up with her changing moods.

Had they made the deal on the guitar? He couldn't decide, but she was standing up, still watching, waiting. And footsteps in the hall meant they were about to be interrupted, probably by Jolynn coming to find her little helper.

"Tell me when, and I'll be there."

"Friday. And afterward Jolynn is having a little party for me. Here, so you can be at that, too."

"Lizzie, I don't think your…"

Jolynn walked through the door, her coral lipstick bright and her smile welcoming. "There's my girl. Are you ready to do laundry, Lizzie Lou?"

"I'm ready. I was just telling Chad why I'm really working for you."

Jolynn hugged the girl tight, and tears slid down her cheeks. "Lizzie, you're trouble with a big old T, but

you've got the biggest heart of any kid I know. Doesn't she, Chad?"

He was a little choked up himself. "Yeah, she sure does."

Lizzie whispered in Jolynn's ear, and Jolynn tossed him another smile. "Well, now, that's real nice."

Lizzie whispered again.

"Of course he can come to the party. He's a part of the family now, isn't he?"

A part of the family. Jolynn's, not Isabelle's.

A truck pulled into the parking lot of the garage. Isabelle told herself she was being paranoid, thinking it was Chad's. She couldn't tell one engine from another. She wasn't a dog. She definitely wasn't going to go running to greet him.

She finished pouring the quart of oil that would complete the oil change on the car she was taking care of and pretended she didn't think it was him walking through the double doors. But he was whistling "Silent Night," and he was the only person she knew with boots that new when she peeked through the crack between the hood and the car frame.

"Hey." She grabbed a rag and wiped her hands as she stepped out into clear view of the man standing next to the car. He'd definitely caught her in a moment when she didn't feel beautiful. Her gray coveralls were grease-stained, and she knew without looking that she probably had a smudge on her cheek, or forehead. Maybe both.

"Hello. I came to give you a message." He stepped a few feet closer, and he wasn't dirty or stained. He was

wearing new jeans with his new boots, and a new white button-up shirt. He didn't smell like grease; he smelled like soap and cologne, the kind that made a woman want to hug him, to get close and enjoy the way his arms would feel holding her tight.

She needed to go home and burn her romance novels. He smiled, and she nearly melted. Why this guy? Why now? Those were questions she needed answers for.

"What's the message?" She got the words out, and she kept wiping her hands to give herself something to think about other than Chad Daniels.

"Your daughter is working late. Jolynn had a lot of dusting to do. They asked me to come down here and let you know that. And also, I thought we might have that real dinner out. You know, the kind with two people sitting at a table together."

Isabelle tossed the rag in the bucket with the others that she'd have to wash later. "You know they're setting us up, right?"

"I kind of thought they might be, but it was getting pretty dusty around the house, and Larry is at an auto auction in Springfield. I thought it might be a good idea to get out."

"I don't know."

"I have to eat. You have to eat. We might as well go out and get something. Jolynn said the special tonight is some kind of chicken pasta."

"I'm not really dressed for going out." She looked down at the coveralls. "I mean, I have clothes to change into, but…"

He grinned, and then he winked. "If we stand here

long enough, I think you'll come up with plenty of excuses for why you can't do this. I think the old excuses, the ones about your daughter needing you at home with her, are starting to lose their validity. She's not at home. She's growing up. Maybe it's your turn to do something for yourself."

If only he hadn't said that. "Chad, it isn't my turn. I still have a twelve-year-old daughter to raise. It's her turn to live, to find her future, to be happy and taken care of. It's her turn to have the life I always dreamed of having."

He sighed and nodded. "Okay, you're right. I've never been a parent. I'm kind of rusty at the whole dating scene myself and what not to say to a woman, especially a woman who is also a mom. I can tell you this—you have a great kid. You're a great mom. You have to eat, and she's already eating with Jolynn."

Isabelle's heart caved. "You make valid points. But it isn't easy, this letting-go thing."

"You have to start, because her growing up isn't going to stop."

"Okay, let me change."

She wouldn't say it was a date. She couldn't do that, not yet. It would take her a while to come to terms with the fact that she'd said yes.

"Shall we walk?" he asked through the door as she changed into clean clothes and washed her face and arms. She didn't have makeup with her, or even perfume. At least she had some lotion that made her feel a little feminine.

"It's only two blocks. I think walking is a good idea. And it isn't freezing cold today."

"The lights will be pretty in the park."

And romantic. Christmas lights, a gorgeous man, and she was wearing wool socks and work boots. So much for romance.

This wasn't the way it happened in movies. But then again, this wasn't romance, either. This was a nice guy taking her to dinner. Her stomach clenched and tied itself in knots. She leaned against the wall, taking a few deep breaths.

"Isabelle?"

"I'll be right out." She rubbed lotion on her arms. And then she looked in the mirror, at a reflection that showed a woman who wasn't getting any younger. Fine lines were starting to appear at the corners of her eyes. Without makeup, she looked pale.

She opened the door and smiled, and he smiled back. He didn't look shocked, or even sorry that he'd asked her to dinner.

Of course he didn't. It was just dinner, nothing more.

Chad reached for Isabelle's hand as they walked out of the garage, but he changed his mind. She had her heart locked up tighter than Fort Knox, and those walls told him she wasn't ready for holding his hand as they walked down the sidewalk of Main Street in Gibson, Missouri.

"You're buying the Berman farm?" she asked as they passed the park. It was lit up with the Nativity, and around the park were the lighted wire frames of the three wise men, camels, angels and shepherds. A speaker, probably hooked up to the fire station, played Christmas music.

The Berman farm—a house with a wraparound porch strung with lights and a tree twinkling in the window of the living room. Today Lizzie had shared Isabelle's dreams with him, dreams of learning to play the guitar. Dreams she'd given up on because she'd had a daughter to raise and her daughter's dreams to take care of.

He hadn't ever been the guy that thought too much about his own dreams, not until he'd started getting letters from Gibson. Until then he'd been pretty content with his military career and single life.

"Yes, I'm buying it." He'd already signed an offer for the farm. But he'd also been contacted by the army, asking him to reenlist.

"You don't seem too thrilled." She glanced up at him, a sweet face devoid of makeup and beautiful because she knew who she was.

"I am." He gave in to the urge and reached for her hand. She looked down at their hands, but she didn't pull away. "I'm buying a used stock trailer from Jay Black-horse, and a friend of his, Cody, is selling me some cattle and a horse."

Did she look wistful, like maybe she had more than one dream, the dream of playing the guitar? Maybe the guitar had been an easy dream to talk about, and to let go of?

"Sounds wonderful." Yes, that was wistfulness in her tone.

They were walking up the sidewalk to the Hash-it-Out, and he could smell the special fried chicken; Isabelle's hand was no longer in his, and he understood why—because Gibson was a small town, and people talked.

He opened the door for her, and she walked through,

a little antsy. She waited for him inside. Of course people would stare. He was new in town, and she was the widowed mother of Lizzie, and she didn't date.

Because she had loved her husband too much to let her heart love again? He had spent a lot of time thinking about that, and he thought about it now as the hostess led them to a corner booth. Maybe she had just gotten too busy with work, life and Lizzie to make room in her heart for a man?

She sat down across from him, clasping her hands on the scarred tabletop, once black Formica, now scratched and faded. The seats of the booth were lumpy, and his even had a piece of gray duct tape covering a tear in the vinyl. It wasn't the most romantic restaurant in the world, but he thought it might be his favorite.

He enjoyed breakfast the best, when farmers and retirees gathered at the tables together, having coffee, biscuits and gravy, and usually a good ration of gossip.

"Why are you smiling?" Isabelle was fiddling with the napkin, running slim fingers over the crease she'd made in it.

"Thinking of this restaurant, the people who come here. I think it's at the top of my list of places to eat."

She laughed at that. "The Hash-it-Out? Not that it isn't great. And Jolynn does make a great apple pie, but really?"

"Really."

The waitress headed their way, slipping past a couple of guys in cowboy hats and dusty boots who flirted as she walked past them. She knocked the hat off one with red hair and told him to go back on the road.

Chad turned his cup over for the waitress to fill. The

woman was young and her makeup was too dark, but her eyes were kind. She smiled at Isabelle. "Well, Isabelle Grant, couldn't you find a better place to go on a Monday night date?"

"It isn't a date." Isabelle's eyelids lowered, and she glanced back at the menu in her hands. "We're just friends. I'm going to have a chef salad."

He glanced up as the waitress gave him a knowing look and mumbled, "Uh-huh."

After he gave his order, the waitress walked away, giving one last look over her shoulder at the cowboy with the red hair, the one who had been teasing her.

"Your daughter invited me to her dance recital."

Isabelle looked up and set down the cup of coffee she'd been stirring creamer into. "Oh, that's sweet of her."

"Do you mind?"

She bit down on her bottom lip, and then she shook her head.

"I don't mind. Of course we'd love it if you could be there."

"She also invited me to Jolynn's party." He sipped black coffee and then set his cup down. "I'm sorry, I can tell her no."

"Why would you do that?"

"Because I don't want you to be uncomfortable. Here I am, in your life because of a Christmas letter your daughter wrote to me last year, and now I'm at recitals, parties, and sitting across from you at dinner."

"I could have said no, but I didn't." She put her spoon on a napkin. "I think we agreed that we would go out and see what it was like, the…"

She glanced around, her lip between her teeth. He followed the quick glance, and he knew what she was thinking. People would be listening, wondering what was going on between the two of them. Being at the café together should have been enough of an answer.

"Right, we did agree to try this." He winked. "So far it isn't bad, is it?" He wanted a smile from her, something that said she felt it, too, the unexplainable connection. First date, he reminded himself.

"No, it isn't bad, but let's avoid the mistletoe." She shot a glance at the ceiling fan in the center of the room, and he saw it hanging there, from the light.

Avoiding the mistletoe was the last promise he wanted to make, so he winked and she blushed.

When they left the restaurant an hour later, he was still wondering how to get her back under that little twig of mistletoe.

Chapter Six

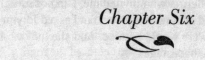

"What have you decided about dance camp?" Mrs. Teague, the owner of Gibson DanceTastic walked next to Isabelle as they left the dressing room where the dancers were waiting for the recital to begin.

Isabelle shrugged at the question. "I don't know yet. I'm saving money, but a lot can happen in six months. I don't want her to be disappointed."

Mrs. Teague patted Isabelle's arm. "Honey, she'll understand. I just wish there was a way that I could help."

"You're already helping. Where else could the girls get ballet lessons from someone with your experience for what you charge?"

"I'm sure there are places." Mrs. Teague's gaze shot past Isabelle, and she nodded at someone standing behind her. "Can we help you?"

"I…" A male voice, hesitant and kind of shy. Not at all the way he normally sounded. "I have flowers for Lizzie."

Isabelle turned, smiling because Chad was a little

red in the face and held the flowers like they were going to bite him.

"You didn't have to bring flowers." She narrowed the distance between them—two steps, and they were close enough for her to smell the roses.

"This one is for you." He handed her a pink rose that was wrapped separate from the other bouquet. "For the mother of the ballerina who invited me. I'm not sure if there is some kind of dance etiquette, but I asked Jolynn, and she said flowers would be nice. And she told me I could bring them backstage."

Jolynn, the troublemaker. Isabelle lifted the rose he'd given her and inhaled the sweet fragrance. "It's beautiful, but we have to go now. They're ready to start."

"The flowers?" He held them in his hand like a club.

"Relax, you can give them to her after the performance. You act as if you've never given a girl flowers before."

He blinked a few times. "Wow, now that you mention it, I don't know if I have. Maybe in high school. Doesn't the guy always get the girl a corsage or something for the prom?"

"I don't know."

She'd never gone to prom, or to a school dance. She swallowed the lump in her throat, leftover pain, bad memories of a childhood that had been spent fighting to survive.

"You don't know?"

She shot him a look and kept walking. They needed to be in their seats, and she didn't have time for him to be clueless now. "We need to hurry."

"Lead the way." He switched the flowers to his left

hand and reached for her hand, holding it tight as they hurried down the hall and through double doors into the gymnasium.

"I have seats up front, next to Jolynn and Larry."

The lights went out. She picked up speed, and they reached the seats just as the lights on the stage came on, pink, yellow and green. She slid in next to Jolynn, and Chad sat next to her.

Next to her. She peeked a glance at him, and he was watching her. He smiled and winked.

No one had ever had that seat next to her. It was reserved for family, and she always brought Jolynn and Larry, sometimes one of the other waitresses at the Hash-it-Out. Tonight it was Chad, and as Lizzie danced across the stage, he applauded as if she were his own, as if that girl on the stage was the most special person in the world. And Isabelle knew that Lizzie saw, that she heard, and that it made a difference.

Not for the first time, she wondered what had made Lizzie write those letters. Was it for Isabelle, because Lizzie didn't want her mom to be lonely? Or was it for Lizzie, because she wanted a man sitting in that seat next to her mom?

The thought ached deep inside as Isabelle watched her daughter, graceful, beautiful and so good. Isabelle's throat tightened, and she bit down on her lip, fighting the tears. A tissue was pushed into her hand. She smiled at Jolynn who had a hankie to wipe her own eyes.

"She's a great kid, Is." Jolynn's arm went around Isabelle's shoulder, and the hug felt great, lessening some of the pain that had sneaked up on her.

She nodded and watched her daughter through eyes that watered, leaving the vision of girls in black and red a little blurry and soft.

As the dance ended, Chad stood, the lone ovation, clapping loud. Lizzie beamed, her smile growing, because this time the man applauding was there for her. Around the gymnasium people stood, joining his ovation.

Isabelle finally took the flowers from him, for fear they'd be squashed. One pink petal had already floated to the floor in his exuberance.

"She's wonderful," he leaned to whisper.

"I know." And it felt good to share that with someone. Someone who didn't have to see how special her daughter was. But he did.

And her heart didn't have to see that as something meaningful, but it did.

"Can I give her the flowers now?"

"Stop being so impatient. She'll be out in just a minute, and you can give them to her then."

"Hey, you two, Larry and I are going to head back to the house and get things ready for the party. Chad, do you want to go with us, or ride with Is and Lizzie?"

"I…" He shot her a questioning look. "Isabelle?"

"You can ride with us."

"Okay, see you kids back at the house." Larry winked at Chad as he and Jolynn walked away.

Isabelle thought about asking what that wink meant, but why bother? She knew how people were. They were always trying to marry her off to someone. And a traitorous voice whispered that Chad wasn't a bad someone.

* * *

If someone had told Chad a year ago that he'd be in Gibson, Missouri, attending a dance recital, he would have laughed. A year ago he had planned to reenlist at the end of his tour. He had planned on four years in Germany, doing a little traveling, maybe some skiing.

Instead, he was walking through the Gibson middle-school gymnasium with three pink roses for Lizzie. He had led soldiers, faced enemies and lived with the thought of death and danger. But this one kid had changed his life. He was in Gibson, not Germany. He had a farm, and an appointment to talk about reenlisting.

"There she is." Isabelle pointed, and he followed the gesture, seeing Lizzie as she walked into the lobby, dressed in jeans and a sweatshirt, a bag over her shoulder and her face freshly washed.

"Mom, Chad." She hurried toward them, and he faltered a little, because he was one of the two people she was smiling for, hurrying toward.

That made him a part of her life, in a way he hadn't really thought about before. He was the person standing next to her mom. He had cheered for her after the performance. He had flowers, a little less perfect now, but her eyes were wide as he held them out. She brought them to her face, then she threw her arms around him, hugging him hard. He faltered a little as he hugged her back, and his gaze connected with Isabelle's in a moment that meant everything.

When he drove into Gibson at the first of the month, what had he thought about this journey, his reason for

being here? He'd told himself it was about finding a home, a place to settle down, some land.

Maybe it had been about Isabelle and Lizzie; maybe it had been about the land. Now it felt as if it was more about Isabelle and her daughter, less about land. But if he reenlisted?

He wasn't sure he could leave them, or leave Gibson. Not with Christmas just a couple of weeks away.

"You okay?"

He smiled at Isabelle. "Yeah, I'm good."

"We should go." She slipped an arm around Lizzie. "Ready?"

"Yep, I'm ready."

Chad walked next to them, sharing in a moment that probably shouldn't have been his. But he was a part of it, and he wanted more; more moments, more of Isabelle in his life.

Brisk cold greeted them as they walked out the doors of the school. Snow flurries were falling, light and feathery, barely visible. Chad wanted a real snow, the kind that piled up. The weatherman had promised maybe an inch, no more.

"Do you want to drive?" Isabelle tossed him her keys, and he had to think fast, putting his hand up to catch them.

"Sure, why not?"

Lizzie laughed. "It isn't even a real snow, just fool's snow, and she won't get behind the wheel. She can fix a car or change the oil, but drive on roads that might get slick, that she won't do."

"It isn't nice to make fun of your mother." Isabelle kissed her daughter's head. "Get in the car."

Chad unlocked the doors and opened the back door for Lizzie, the front door for Isabelle. She smiled up at him before sliding into the car. He walked around to the driver's side and got behind the wheel of the aging sedan. When he started it, he smiled.

"Surprised?" Isabelle clicked her seat belt into place. "I'm a mechanic, remember?"

"It sounds great."

"It is great. It's twenty years old, but I bought it from a sweet lady who kept it in her garage most of the time. She drove it to church on Sunday and to quilting on Friday. The rest of the time she walked or rode with friends."

It was a cherry of a car. A Lincoln with the original paint, original engine and leather seats. It was a boat, but drove like a new car. Chad wheeled out of the parking lot and headed in the direction of the Pine Tree Inn.

He drove down the now-familiar streets that were lined with trees bare of leaves and houses decorated with lights of all colors. The headlights of the car captured the falling snow, and next to him he could see the reflection of Isabelle Grant, dark-eyed and somber, in the passenger window of the car.

There were half a dozen cars in the driveway of Jolynn's. He pulled into the space next to his truck and parked. He hadn't expected a crowd like this.

"Wow, Jolynn really decorated the place this year." Isabelle stepped out of the car and stared up at the house.

Chad walked up next to her, ignoring Lizzie's hidden chuckle as she hurried away from them. "I did this."

"You did this?"

He nodded and surveyed his work. Candy canes, four feet tall, lined the sidewalk. Lights framed the porch and windows. Spiral trees adorned with lights ran the length of the driveway. In the center of the lawn was Jolynn's Nativity.

"I did this. And don't laugh." He reached for her hand.

"I won't laugh." She stopped walking.

It was cold, and the snow was coming down a little harder. Chad stood next to her, wondering why they were standing outside when there was hot coffee and cocoa inside. But he wasn't going to complain, not with her hand in his.

He thought about kissing her, and wondered if her lips would be cold. He wondered if she would slip her arms around him, or stand still, holding her breath. Or if she'd turn away.

With snow falling and Christmas lights twinkling all around them, he bent, touching his lips to hers. She held her breath, but her lips were warm and tasted like the mint gloss he'd seen her swipe across them when they got into her car. She moved, touching her lips to his cheek, and then she stepped back. Her eyes were closed, and a tear slipped down her cheek. He wondered if it was the good kind that came from overwhelming but happy emotions. Or if it was a tear of regret.

"Isabelle, I'd like to take you out again. Maybe somewhere a little more romantic than the Hash-it-Out."

"Chad, please don't."

"Don't what?"

"I don't date. I mean, I haven't dated in years. It feels like a tug-of-war, being pulled between building a rela-

tionship and raising my daughter. Lizzie can't take the backseat to a relationship."

"I would never ask that of you."

"I know, but my childhood." She pulled the lip balm out of her pocket and neatly swiped her lips again. "I was the child who was forgotten when my mother dated. She dated a lot."

"Isabelle, I know that you're a package deal. I would never forget Lizzie. How could I?"

"I'm glad you understand. Sometimes I don't know if I understand." She wiped at her eyes. "I don't know if I've ever had a grown-up relationship."

"I know you loved your husband."

"Yes, I loved him."

He hadn't expected his heart to tighten the way it did when she said those words. She had been another man's wife. His heart had never been involved, not like that.

"We should go in." He said the only thing he could think of at the moment. It was cold, and the air was damp. Isabelle was shivering in front of him, and he knew that everyone inside would be speculating over what was going on between them.

"That's probably a good idea." She spoke softly, slipping her hand back in his.

Isabelle managed a smile as they walked through the doors of Jolynn's house and into a world that was Christmas and family and laughter. There were more than a dozen people milling around the large living room, standing in small groups, talking, laughing. Isabelle searched the room for her daughter and didn't

see her. But Lacey and Jay Blackhorse stood in the corner near the piano, baby Rachel in Lacey's arms.

They were a shining example of a couple that had found the perfect person to spend a lifetime with.

It had to be the Christmas music, the lights, the many smiling friends that made Isabelle want to believe in forever with someone who would love her, someone who wouldn't hurt her. As she turned to go in search of her daughter, her gaze connected with Chad's, and he winked.

That's how she missed the tabby cat slinking across the room. Isabelle tripped over the animal, falling slightly forward and righting herself just before she made contact with a table that held a vase of red roses. Out of the corner of her eyes, she caught a glimpse of Chad as he started for her.

The cat she tripped over yowled and ran under the burgundy sofa.

"You okay?"

She didn't look up, didn't meet Chad's gaze. She wondered if he would be concerned or amused. She replayed the moment in her mind and then looked up at him, smiling. Because it really was funny.

"I'm fine."

"And graceful."

"Very." And she was falling over more than a cat. She was falling for a smile, for a man who seemed to know the right things to say.

And that scared her. She had never fallen. She'd been comfortable with Dale, and comfortable with her life here in Gibson, raising her daughter and being a part of this community.

Now, though, she had other thoughts about her future and about life after Lizzie was grown and gone.

"I'm going to see if Jolynn needs help in the kitchen."

He shrugged and stayed next to her as she left the room. As they passed through the doorway, Isabelle looked up, seeing the mistletoe tacked to the wood frame. She sidestepped, and Chad reached for her hand, trying to pull her back.

She couldn't let him do that. She'd fallen once tonight, maybe twice; she didn't need to fall a third time.

"I think we'll avoid the mistletoe." She slid her hand out of his, careful to not bring up the fact that there hadn't been mistletoe outside, just light snow and lights.

"I'll help you help Jolynn."

They walked down the hall aglow with candles in the wall sconces, and his hand reached for hers again. Her heart didn't know whether to freeze up or beat in time to "Winter Wonderland."

She needed to get a grip. He'd come here looking for a woman who wasn't real, who was just the fictional version of Lizzie's mom. Reality was so different.

"You know, I'm not the person in Lizzie's letters." She stopped in the hall.

"Really? I thought you were, Isabelle."

"I'm Isabelle, but I'm real, not the version my daughter fed you. I'm not confident or funny. I'm sure she painted a different picture, tinted everything in pretty colors."

"I think she was honest. She showed me the Isabelle who loves her daughter and cares about the people in her life."

"But I'm the Isabelle who has chapped hands from doing dishes. And a gray hair." She pulled it out for him to see. She knew exactly where it was, because she'd considered yanking it out. "Three days a week I smell like car grease. Four days a week I smell like fried chicken. On Sundays I get to put on lotion and smell like flowers and sunshine."

"I noticed." He leaned close to her ear. "I think you have beautiful hands. I love fried chicken. I especially love flowers and sunshine. And I like the real Isabelle."

She pulled away, because his lips were close to hers. "You like Christmas. You love Gibson, the lights, the people. It's all manufactured emotion because of those things and the fact that you're finding a home to settle down in."

A throat cleared. "Are the two of you going to lurk in my hall all night?"

"Jolynn. We were coming to see if you need any help."

Jolynn nodded her head, but her eyes narrowed, and she smiled a little. "Of course I could use help."

Isabelle hurried away from temptation and into the brightly lit kitchen. The big room had light hickory cabinets, dark granite countertops and stainless appliances. It was a dream kitchen. Tonight the counters were loaded down with food.

Chad walked in a minute after her, tall and not flustered. Since his arrival, his dark hair had grown out just a little. He looked as good in a plaid button-up shirt as he had in that camouflage uniform.

He sat on one of the bar stools and watched as she cut a pie.

Jolynn untied the apron she wore. "I'm going to take a pot of hot cocoa out to the crowd, and then we'll herd them in here to have food. Don't stay in here, Is. This is your little girl's party."

"I'm not going to hide in the kitchen, just going to get a few things done." She glanced toward the sink full of dishes. "And wash a few dishes."

Jolynn was already gone, but Chad had heard. He left his stool and walked around to the sink. As she finished cutting the last pie, he started the dishwater.

"What are you doing?" She walked up next to him.

"I'm going to help wash dishes."

"Really?"

He grabbed the sprayer attached to the sink. "Stop sounding so surprised, or I'll spray you. I do know how to wash dishes."

"I'm sure you do."

He faced her, putting the sprayer back in place. "Isabelle, I do know the real you. Maybe not as well as if I'd spent time here, but I know you. I know that you like it when people offer to help do the dishes."

"True, but the letter was from Lizzie, and she's the one who really likes it when someone else helps me do the dishes. It means she gets out of doing them." She rolled up her sleeves, unable to meet his dark gaze. He didn't let her get away with avoiding him. He touched her cheek, turning her face so that their gazes connected.

"I know that you love your daughter more than anything. And I know that she knows that, too."

"What else did she tell you?" But did she really want to know what secrets her daughter might have shared?

"I know that you love romance, but only in books and movies."

Okay, that was embarrassing.

"I know that you miss Dale. And Lizzie knows that you still cry at night. I know that you counted on him to always be here for you. I'm sorry."

Isabelle looked away, because this had gone too far. It had started out as something fun and light, but the emotion felt heavy. It cloaked her heart, weighing her down.

"I'm sorry, too. But those are small details. And Dale—" She took the dishrag from him and scrubbed a pan. How did she tell him about Dale? "Dale and I were best friends."

"I've heard that's how to have a great relationship."

She shook her head. "We loved each other, but we weren't in love. We were best friends who promised to keep each other safe. He kept me safe."

She glanced up, wanting to see the look on his face, to know how he took that revelation. Her childhood was a life he couldn't understand.

"I think I understand." He took the pan from her and rinsed it. "It's good to have someone who never lets you down."

She grabbed a bowl to wash. This was so hard, harder than anything she'd done in a long time. "So, now you know the things about my life that my daughter couldn't have shared with you. And I know that you're planning to reenlist. Is there really a point to pursuing this? I mean, you're going to leave."

She had repeated gossip she'd heard at the diner, something she'd promised herself she'd never do. She

started to apologize but loud voices carried down the hall and a minute later they were joined by the rest of the party. Lizzie was at the front of the group. She glanced in Isabelle's direction, not smiling. Isabelle wondered if it was her imagination, or if those were tears shimmering in her daughter's eyes.

Chapter Seven

It was nearly eleven that night when Isabelle and Lizzie got home. Isabelle was wiped out. She wanted her bed. She wanted to not have to get up at six the following morning. As they walked through the front door, Lizzie hurried out of the room without saying anything.

She'd been quiet all night and hadn't talked during the ride home. Isabelle tossed her purse on the table and went to the kitchen, lit only with a bulb over the sink. She turned on the overhead lights and found a clean glass in the dishwasher.

"Here." Lizzie tossed a small stack of letters on the counter. "These are his letters. If you read them, you'll know who he is and how much he cares about the people in his life. He's someone you can trust. And I don't think he's going to leave."

"What?" Isabelle didn't know what surprised her more, the challenge to read the letters or this new attitude of

her daughter's. They'd always been close, always seen eye to eye on most things.

The challenge in Lizzie's eyes was what Isabelle had seen when three-year-old Lizzie wanted candy that Isabelle wouldn't give her.

"Mom, you can't live your life for me. I'm not always going to be here. I can't be your excuse for not getting involved, for not dating."

"Is that how you see me?" Isabelle filled her glass with water and turned back to face her daughter. "You think I'm avoiding relationships."

"I think you love romance that is safe. The kind in books or on TV. I think you're afraid."

"I'm not afraid."

"Yeah, well, I'm praying you fall in love with Chad." And that was the twelve-year-old, with her chin up and her eyes overflowing with unshed tears. "That's what I want for Christmas. I want a dad."

Isabelle took a step toward her daughter but knew that Lizzie wouldn't welcome a hug, not yet. "Oh, Liz, I want to give you everything. I can do the easy things, like ballet lessons and church camp. I might someday be able to afford dance camp. But I can't give you a dad for Christmas. You can't pick a dad that way. And you can't force two people to fall in love."

"No, but what if this is what God planned? What if that letter to Chad was God putting this all into place for us?"

Isabelle didn't have an answer. How many times had she told her daughter to trust God's plan and to see God in the unexpected things that happened in their lives?

And now something unexpected had happened, and Isabelle didn't have an answer.

"Lizzie, I don't know God's plan. But I'm sure we'll know it when it happens. As much as you want this, you can't make it happen."

"Read his letters. Please." Lizzie kissed Isabelle on the cheek and walked down the hall.

He was going to reenlist. Lizzie had to get that.

Isabelle could hear the normal sounds of her daughter getting ready for bed. Water running as she brushed her teeth and then washed her face, the alarm clock being set and then the radio coming on. She bit down on her bottom lip, trying to make sense of what had happened to their lives, their relationship. She touched the small stack of letters from Chad Daniels, lieutenant colonel, U.S. Army.

Closing her eyes, she could see his face, his smile, the kindness in his eyes. She could remember what it felt like when he held her, and when their lips touched.

She remembered what life felt like when someone hurt her. She remembered the pain of abuse. She remembered the foster family that had decided to leave the state and to not take her with them. Dale had been the constant in her growing-up years.

And then he'd been gone. But she'd had Lizzie to raise and Jolynn to lean on. She'd found faith and a Heavenly Father who never walked away and who accepted her as she was, faults and all. She didn't have to be the perfect child to gain His love.

So where did Chad fit into their lives?

* * *

Chad drove past his farm the next morning, slowing at the drive, but then going on, because he didn't want to think about what if this had been a mistake. The farm, coming here, Isabelle. He'd never realized before, but he was pretty bad at life outside of the military. That had become clear in the last couple of weeks. In his job he'd known what to do every day. He knew what was expected of him. He knew the people around him and what they wanted from him.

Not that surprises didn't happen. He was trained to handle the unexpected.

Nothing in his training had prepared him for Isabelle and Lizzie Grant. They were a package deal. That was a heavy thought and one that a guy couldn't take lightly, especially when he had just gotten out of the army and he had been single all of his adult life.

He had lived twenty-three years of having his days, weeks and months planned. He liked being organized. He liked knowing what tomorrow held for him. And yet there was something about this civilian life, the not knowing, that challenged him.

He pulled up in front of the Hash-it-Out and parked, but he didn't get out. This town had been in Lizzie's letters, luring him here, to community and people he knew only from her descriptions. Being here had added dimension to their personalities.

Someone rapped on the truck window. He jumped a little and turned. Jay Blackhorse nodded toward the diner. Chad pulled his key out of the ignition and followed the other man, a cowboy who had always been

a cowboy. Chad felt a little like an impostor in his boots that were still new and unscuffed.

"What's up with you this morning?" Jay opened the door and walked through, holding it for Chad to follow.

"I have a few things to think through." Chad thanked the hostess who led them to one of the few empty tables. Conversation droned in the busy restaurant, and the people he knew waved or said hello.

It hadn't taken long to become a part of this community.

Jay scooted his chair out from the table and sat down. Chad did the same, turning his cup so the waitress could fill it with coffee. She smiled at him like she knew a secret, and when she walked away, it was as if she owned the whole world.

Chad shook his head, wishing he knew the secrets she knew. Maybe it would help him make the right choice. But prayer was probably a better option.

"Jay, I'm thinking about that offer to reenlist."

"You can't take care of cattle if you're in Germany."

"No, that's something I can't do."

"If this is about…"

Chad raised his hand. There were too many people sitting too close to them, and he didn't want the rumors to get started. Or get out of control. Since Isabelle knew, it was a pretty sure thing there were already people talking. How could they not? He was the guy that came to town because of letters a twelve-year-old had written. A twelve-year-old posing as her mother.

"This is about me not being sure where I'm supposed to go. I'm going to drive down to the base and talk to

some people. And my parents called and asked me to fly down there for Christmas."

Fly to Florida, where the temperatures would hover around sixty degrees, and Christmas dinner would be at the clubhouse restaurant. That didn't appeal to him at all.

The only real tradition his family had was the conference call every Christmas. That was the one time of the year they touched base and caught up on what was happening in each other's lives.

The thought left him a little cold this year, especially with memories of Friday night still fresh. Jolynn's house, the fresh-fallen snow and people who weren't related but loved one another. He'd had times like that in the army with the people in his unit. In the military they did become family to one another.

He hadn't had kids of his own, but there were a few soldiers he felt as if he'd helped to raise. And he'd learned from a few of them, too.

"Well, you know you have people here who would like to spend Christmas with you." Jay leaned back in his chair, picking up the menu to browse. And Chad knew that the menu didn't matter. Jay had the same breakfast every morning. He had poached eggs, a slice of ham and juice.

Chad had gone for a two-mile run that morning, and he felt a little better about ordering the biscuits and gravy that he had every morning. The gravy was the real stuff, not a powdered mix. The biscuits were Jolynn's specialty.

"I know that I can stay." He returned to their conversation after the waitress left. "But I need to make sure this is what I'm supposed to do."

The cowbell on the door clanged. He shot a look in that direction, and almost everything he believed to be right fled, because Isabelle Grant was beautiful, even in jeans and a T-shirt, her hair in a braid.

"Yeah, you're not a guy whose guts are tied up in a neat little bow, compliments of a waitress and her daughter." Jay laughed, not caring about the look Chad shot him. "I think maybe you're running scared."

Nothing was tied up in a neat little bow. And if he said he wasn't scared, he would sound like a four-year-old arguing that the dark didn't scare him.

Chad barely spoke to her that morning at the Hash-it-Out. When Isabelle got home, she was still reliving the look in his eyes, the way he'd said goodbye when he left. The look had been one of confusion. She knew how he felt.

She didn't have time to think about it. That was what she'd been telling herself, and she knew it was true. Trying to figure out a man was exhausting. Raising a daughter, also exhausting. Missing him—she wasn't even going to go there. She wouldn't miss him when he was gone.

Tonight she had to wrap Christmas presents while Lizzie was working at Jolynn's. It was the perfect opportunity to get something accomplished. She made herself a pot of coffee and walked into the living room. But the tree was there, the one Chad had helped decorate. She stopped at the doorway between the dining area and living room, looking at the tree, the star on top. God had planned the birth of the baby they cele-

brated each Christmas. She closed her eyes, knowing He had a plan for her life, for her future. He knew the emptiness in her heart and the way it felt different now, because of the man who had shown up in their lives just a few weeks earlier.

A man who might be leaving to go back into the army.

Pointless, these thoughts were pointless. She hadn't planned on a man in her life. She hadn't invited this one to show up. And she knew that she'd be fine when he was gone.

She went into the bedroom to drag out the bags of gifts, wrapping paper and tape. She glanced at the letters on her nightstand and glanced away, resisting the temptation to read them.

Instead, she dumped the gifts on the bed. Most were small items that Lizzie had wanted. Hair stuff, face stuff and nail stuff. A cute purse and jeans from the mall—a special treat on their budget. Girls were easy that way. Lizzie was easy. She'd never asked for a lot.

And she'd missed out on so much.

But not love. Isabelle reminded herself of that one major detail. Her daughter had never had to wonder if she was loved. Lizzie had never felt that aching emptiness of rejection.

But she wouldn't be going to dance camp, not this year.

Isabelle picked up the tech gadget that Lizzie had wanted for the last year. Downloadable music. She shook her head, because the world had changed a lot in fifteen years. Isabelle had wanted a boom box as a kid.

Christmas gifts were a special part of the holiday, but feeling loved, that was what counted. Isabelle knew

from experience. As a foster child she'd been given gifts, sometimes dozens. But the gifts had often, not always, been empty gestures without love.

She knew that Lizzie had written that first letter to a soldier because she had wanted some young man in Iraq to know that someone cared about him, someone was praying for him.

She remembered the two of them praying together that Lizzie's letter would reach the right soldier. That memory was hard to relive, especially with his letters in her hands. Letters he'd intended for her.

The door opened. She jumped a little and hurried to cover the gifts. But they were all wrapped. Lizzie laughed.

"What are you so jumpy for, the letters or the presents you're trying to hide?" The cheeky kid stepped into the room, eyeing the gifts.

"Shouldn't you be at work?"

"It's six o'clock, time to be home and have dinner with my mom. Are we having soup?"

"No, I thought I'd order pizza."

"Wow, a special occasion?"

"No, a guilty mom who didn't get dinner cooked."

"So, you're going to read the letters?" Lizzie sat on the edge of the bed, smoothing the patchwork quilt that an older lady in church had made. One for Isabelle, and one for Lizzie.

"I have to order pizza."

"I'll order it in thirty minutes. That gives you time to read the letters." Lizzie kissed her cheek. "He's a pretty neat guy, Mom."

Isabelle nodded, because she already knew that.

Lizzie slipped out of the room, closing the door behind her. For twelve she was too grown up. Of course, she was nearly thirteen. Lizzie liked to remind her of that. As if Isabelle could forget.

She slid the letter out of the first envelope. She skimmed it, knowing she'd have to read between the lines because a lot of the letter seemed to answer questions that Lizzie had asked. She started at the top, sitting on the edge of her bed as she read.

Lizzie must have asked him if he was a Christian. Isabelle smiled, because her daughter would do that. He answered that he was a new Christian. He hadn't been raised in church, but had attended on holidays. He explained that when he started attending services, some of his buddies accused him of turning to God because he was afraid. He didn't care that they thought faith made him weak. He thought that faith made him stronger. He started to take a good look at the men of faith he knew. They were all strong and courageous. And then he read the Bible and saw that the men in the Bible who called on God were anything but weak.

He signed the letter telling her that it was nearly Easter and he would someday send her sand from Iraq, because it was the land where Bible history happened.

He had given Isabelle that sand the day he showed up on her doorstep.

Isabelle slipped the letter back into the envelope and pulled out the next, and the next, and the next. And through the letters she saw the man her daughter had seen. He was strong. He poured out thoughts about the

younger people in his unit and wanting to get them home safe. He talked about not having children, but he had always thought, well, someday.

He told her that he would love to meet Lizzie, because she was the type of girl any parent would be proud of.

Isabelle stared at the closed door, the door that girl had walked through thirty minutes earlier. She was proud of her daughter. Aggravated with her, because she had brought Chad here without him knowing the truth about them, about her. But still, it had been a sweet thing to do.

It had been what a girl would do if she wanted a dad.

Isabelle rubbed her eyes and leaned back against her pillows. Her daughter wanted a dad. Downloadable music, dance camp and ballet, too, but the real deal, the real thing Lizzie wanted, was a family.

At twelve, Isabelle had wanted the same thing.

But she couldn't welcome Chad in the role of dad *just because*. They weren't paper dolls, where you just grabbed a male figure, dressed him up and gave him the role of husband and dad.

Lizzie needed to understand that there was more to it than that. She put the letters together and slid the rubber band back in place to hold them. When she walked out of her room, she didn't see her daughter.

"Lizzie, are you out here?"

"Yeah, I'm here." She walked out of the utility room, folding a towel. "The pizza will be ready in fifteen minutes."

"Good. Lizzie, sit down." They were in the dining room. Isabelle flipped on the light, and they sat down

at the small dinette with the fake wood top, scarred and nicked from years of use. "Honey, I know that you want a dad. I get it, because I know how much I wanted a real dad. But we can't pick a guy out of a hat and stick him in our lives this way. There's more to relationships than that. A man and woman…"

Lizzie giggled and covered her face. "Oh, Mom, please don't do 'the talk.' Not now, right before pizza. I know that I can't pick the guy for you. But you don't pick guys at all. You don't even seem to see them. So I thought if I put one on your doorstep…"

"He'd be Prince Charming and I'd be Cinderella?"

Lizzie shrugged. "It was worth a try. I think I kind of hoped a Christmas letter would turn into a Christmas miracle."

"Let's leave these things up to God." Isabelle stood and leaned to kiss her daughter's smooth, dark head. "I'll run and get the pizza."

"Okay. Mom, I am sorry."

"I know you are. I love you." Isabelle grabbed her jacket and walked out the front door. It was cold, and the sky had the heavy gray look of winter and snow. Chad loved snow, and he'd never had a home, not a real home.

She had learned from his letters that home was the place they moved into on base after the last officer left. His mom had always turned it into a home, though. Isabelle thought his mother was probably a strong woman.

And his dad—an honorable man who didn't want to miss the programs at school; but all too often, he had. But that explained why Chad had attended Lizzie's

dance recital and why he'd clapped longer and louder than anyone. Because a kid should know that someone was in the audience cheering them on.

And that moment, when she read those words and remembered him that night, cheering for her daughter, that's when her heart had shifted in an unexpected direction and her brain had told her it was too late to deny what she felt for him.

Chapter Eight

"Is, you have a call from Blane at the flea market." Jolynn held out the phone.

"Could you take a message?" Isabelle nodded at her customers, tourists who'd come to the area to shop at flea markets in the smaller towns. She didn't want to walk away when they were about to order their lunch.

"Can do." Jolynn held the phone with her shoulder and wrote something on a piece of paper.

Isabelle finished taking the order and headed for the kitchen. Jolynn met her in the back and handed her the note. "He has something for you to pick up."

"For me to pick up?" Isabelle clipped the order to the holder above the grill and smiled at Mary, the afternoon cook.

"Yes, for you. Go on over and see what it is. I'll hold down the fort."

"But my customers…"

"I'll take care of them and earn you a good tip."

Isabelle shrugged and grabbed her jacket off the hook. "I guess I'll be right back."

As she crossed the street and headed up the block to the flea market, she got the impression that Jolynn knew exactly what was waiting for her there. But that was okay; it was a pretty day to be outside. The weather had warmed to an almost balmy forty-five degrees, and the sun was out. Christmas was just a few days away.

It should have felt good. Christmas always felt good. So why not this year? She didn't want to think about the reason. Or maybe wanted to tell herself that it couldn't be because Chad Daniels had left town, on his way to a base to talk about reenlisting.

Someone had told her that he would lease the farm for a few years if he did reenlist. It seemed a shame to buy a place that was his dream and then walk away from it.

A bell dinged as she walked through the door of the flea market. She smiled at the owner, a man in his fifties who sometimes went to their church. He walked behind the counter and returned with a guitar case.

"I have a gift that was left here for you." He held it out, smiling big, like he was a part of the surprise. "Here's a note."

"This can't be for me." She didn't want to take it, for fear it wouldn't be true. She knew what was in that case. She had picked it up once before, strumming the strings and then putting it down because she wouldn't let herself dream.

"It's yours." He pushed it at her, forcing her to take it. And then she took the note.

She set the guitar case down, leaning it against a

dusty old sofa with gold velvet upholstery. The shop was a mixture of other people's junk and antiques. She sometimes found good stuff in this place: clothes, dishes, even books.

The envelope held a Christmas card. There was a picture of a dog with a Rudolph nose on the front, and she knew that someone had been thinking of Gibson's own Santa when they bought that card. She opened it, her fingers trembling.

> *Because you do so much for everyone else. You deserve to have your dreams come true.*
> Love, Chad and Lizzie.

She whispered the two names signed together on the bottom of the card. She wouldn't cry. She wasn't going to cry. She slipped the card back into the envelope and picked up the guitar, holding it for a minute and not sure what to do with it, with a gift like that.

She was used to socks and body lotion for Christmas, sometimes a sweater. Not a guitar that had cost hundreds of dollars, money she could have used for Lizzie's camp.

"Enjoy it, Isabelle."

She looked up, remembering she wasn't alone.

"I will, thank you." She walked out, this time not hearing the bell, not hearing anything. She walked down the street, feeling numb, and then hurt, and then warm, because two people had done this for her.

She walked through the doors of the Hash-it-Out and back to the kitchen, to the storage room in the back of the building. Jolynn followed her.

"Are you okay?"

A motherly hand on her back. Isabelle nodded, but she didn't turn around, not with tears flooding her vision and her heart trying to find its rhythm again.

"I'm not sure why he did this," Isabelle whispered.

"It was Lizzie's idea."

Isabelle turned, knowing there was an explanation and that it might not be one she wanted to hear. "Okay, I can see it being her idea. She is the idea girl. But the money..."

"Is, the money came from working at my place. She told you she was saving the money for camp. The truth is, she wanted you to have this gift. She wanted you to have something you've always wanted. So she worked for me. And Chad pitched in because he was touched by the fact that she was willing to work for this gift when she wants to go to camp so much."

"But camp. She really wanted to save money for camp. I want her to have camp more than I want this guitar."

"And she wants you to be happy. So don't take that sweetness away from her. Don't lecture her for this, thank her for it. You have a wonderful child who is loving and giving. That's the greatest gift I think a parent could ever receive."

"I think so, too." But this was another way that Lizzie was taking care of her mother. "But I think this shows me something important, too."

Jolynn wiped tears from beneath her eyes, smudging her mascara in the process. "What's that, sweetie?"

"I need to get a life so my daughter will stop thinking she needs to take care of me."

Her thoughts turned, traitorously, to Chad Daniels.

She didn't want to think about the fact that she missed a man who had left town a few days ago and had probably already reenlisted in the military.

"Mom, you like the guitar, right?" Lizzie stood in the center of the living room the day before Christmas Eve, the day before the big Gibson parade. And it was big. People came from all over to view the evening parade. It was the one tourist event the small town could lay claim to.

Isabelle sat on the floor touching up the lace on her daughter's costume for the dance at the end of the parade. The girls who attended DanceTastic would participate in the parade, doing small routines to taped music, but at the end of the parade route, they would do a longer dance.

"Of course I love it." She snipped the thread from the last seam. "And I love you."

"Don't you think it was sweet of Chad to help me buy it?"

Isabelle looked up, meeting the hopeful smile of her daughter. "Yes, it was sweet. It was a kind thing for him to do. Lizzie, you know he's gone, right? He went to talk to people about reenlisting."

"Yeah, I know, but he'll be back. He bought the Berman farm. He wants to raise cattle and have horses."

"I know." Isabelle stood up. "And you look beautiful."

"You're changing the subject."

"Of course I am." Because she wanted Lizzie to be the child, and Isabelle would be the grown-up who took care of her. She wasn't going to tell her daughter how

much her heart hurt because Chad was gone, and that she hadn't expected it to hurt.

She flipped on the television, hoping to change the subject, maybe back to Christmas. "Hey, this is a good movie. Let's make popcorn and watch it."

"It's pretty sad at the end," Lizzie said with certain knowledge because it was a movie they watched every year.

"It has a happy ending."

"Yeah, but it always makes you cry. Why do happy endings do that?"

Isabelle didn't have an answer to that. Maybe because of the hope of dreams coming true? Maybe because everyone wanted to cheer for someone to get the wonderful things they deserved?

A truck rumbled into their driveway. They both hurried to the window, and Isabelle knew they were both thinking of Chad. But it was a delivery van. The guy got out of the truck and carried an envelope to the door.

"You get it." Isabelle patted Lizzie on the back. "I'll make the popcorn."

She was in the kitchen when Lizzie screamed.

Isabelle dropped the bag of popcorn onto the counter and hurried into the living room. Her daughter was standing in the center of the room, tears streaming down her cheeks. The delivery van was backing out of the driveway, and a letter was in Lizzie's trembling hands.

"What is it?" Isabelle took the letter as Lizzie sobbed.

Someone had paid for Lizzie to attend one month of dance camp. That someone was Chad Daniels. The letter was signed with a scrawled *Merry Christmas*.

Chapter Nine

Chad parked his truck and got out. The streets were crowded, lined with people. It was nearly dark. He glanced at his watch. The parade would start in five minutes. That meant he had minutes to find Isabelle. He hurried down the sidewalk, away from Jolynn's, and hopefully in the direction of what he'd been looking for his entire life.

It had taken a dotted line, a signature he had almost signed, before he had realized that he wanted to stay in Gibson. He missed the military and the relationships, the bonds of serving with other men and women.

But if he went back, he'd miss Isabelle and, of course, Lizzie. And he didn't want to miss them. He already missed them.

He hurried down the sidewalk, his step light, his heart hammering in his chest like a man about to go into the danger zone, facing the unknown. On his way home—*home,* he liked the way that sounded—he had thought

of all the right things to say. At the hotel last night he'd even watched a few of those sappy movies she liked so much. He wouldn't admit that to a single person.

But a guy had to know what to say when he faced the woman he loved and wanted to spend the rest of his life with. Especially a woman like Isabelle, a woman who was strong, tender, vulnerable and beautiful.

A woman with a daughter. That would make him a stepdad, if Isabelle ever agreed to marry him. He had bought a half-dozen books on the subject yesterday. In the end he had left them in the hotel. He didn't need to know how to be a stepdad. What Lizzie needed was a *dad*.

He practically ran down Main Street, because he could hear band music in the distance. He glanced at his watch, knowing the parade had just started.

A few hundred feet away he thought he saw her, a woman with dark hair, wearing a plaid jacket. She turned, and it wasn't Isabelle.

Her cell phone. He pushed in her number, and as he waited for her to answer, he kept walking and kept running through his mind what he wanted to say when he saw her. He slipped his left hand into his pocket and smiled.

"Hello." Isabelle stepped away from the crowd that waited at the end of the parade route. She hadn't expected Chad's voice on the other end of the phone, or his number on the caller ID.

She had hoped he would be here for this performance. She wanted to thank him for the guitar. Lizzie wanted to thank him for dance camp.

Even now her eyes flooded with tears when she

thought about his kindness. And how much she hadn't planned on missing him.

"What are you doing?" His voice was soft, and she closed her eyes. She hadn't planned on this feeling. It felt like falling in love for the first time.

"I'm at the parade." She listened, knowing it would only be five minutes before the dancers reached them. Gibson packed a lot into a parade that was a mere one mile long. They had three school bands, the dancers, saddle club, a dozen church floats and the Boy Scouts.

"I thought you might be there." His voice crackled a little as his signal cut out. "Have you seen Lizzie yet?"

"No, I'm at the end of the route, waiting." She peered down Main Street, and she could see the flashing lights of the town police car. "I think they're almost to me. So, did you reenlist?"

"No. I couldn't reenlist."

"Really? Why?" She took a deep breath and closed her eyes.

"Because I realized that as much as I love the military, there's something I love more."

"What?" Was that her voice, sounding breathless?

"You." And he was no longer on the phone. She opened her eyes, and he was standing in front of her, tall and strong, his smile flashing in a face so handsome, so familiar, it felt like she'd known him forever.

"Oh." Yes, that was breathless. And happy endings always made her cry. But she didn't realize that would include her own. "But you hardly know me."

"I know you." He pulled her close. "I know that yellow is your favorite color. I know you like your

coffee with one spoon of sugar and a lot of creamer, but not real cream. I know you love your daughter, and I know that I love her, too. I know that you always cry over happy endings."

She nodded, and tears were streaming down her cheeks. "That part is definitely true."

"I know that I would like the chance to get to know you better, and for you to know me. I also know that next year, I'd like to help decorate your tree again, but I kind of hope that by next Christmas it will be *our* tree."

"I think I might like that, too."

The parade was marching past, and she could see the dancers in the distance.

"I think I might like to kiss you again," Chad whispered in her ear. "I even have mistletoe."

His hand slid into his coat pocket, and he lifted a green sprig into the air. She started to comment, but before she could, he lowered his head and kissed her. Isabelle closed her eyes as he held her close.

"Chad, I love you, too." She leaned against him as her daughter came into sight, dancing to "Silent Night."

He held her close to his side, and they watched Lizzie, together. Together. Isabelle loved that word, because it meant no longer being alone.

* * * * *

Dear Reader

Welcome to Christmas in Gibson, Missouri. I grew up in rural Missouri, and Gibson is every small town that I know. Church, family and tradition are a big part of these communities. It is so easy to get rushed along with the business of Christmas shopping and preparations. For that reason it's important to find those traditions that keep us grounded and help us to focus on what Christmas really means to us and to our families.

I hope you enjoy Chad and Isabelle's Christmas story.

Merry Christmas!

Brenda Minton

QUESTIONS FOR DISCUSSION

1. Isabelle didn't expect to find Chad on her doorstep. How would this surprise challenge her faith and her own thoughts about her future?

2. Isabelle has taught Lizzie to find God in the unexpected things. Is Chad showing up just coincidence, one of those things that happens? Or could it be God's plan, bringing a family together?

3. The people of Gibson have traditions such as the turning on of the Christmas lights and the ceremony in the fire station. How do those things help them to focus on Christmas?

4. Isabelle learned that she doesn't have to be perfect. God loves her, faults and all. How did that change her life?

5. Chad learned that faith made him stronger. How do you think he came to that realization?

6. In life we tend to want to go back to what is comfortable rather than taking a chance on something new. Chad almost reenlists. What pushed him to make that decision, and why was it the wrong thing to do?

*Here's a sneak peek at "Merry Mayhem"
by Margaret Daley,
one of the two riveting suspense stories in the
new collection CHRISTMAS PERIL,
available in December 2009
from Love Inspired® Suspense.*

"Run. Disappear… Don't trust anyone, especially the police."

Annie Coleman almost dropped the phone at her ex-boyfriend's words, but she couldn't. She had to keep it together for her daughter. Jayden played nearby, oblivious to the sheer terror Annie was feeling at hearing Bryan's gasped warning.

"Thought you could get away," a gruff voice she didn't recognize said between punches. "You haven't finished telling me what I need to know."

Annie panicked. What was going on? What was happening to Bryan on the other end? Confusion gripped her in a chokehold, her chest tightening with each inhalation.

"I don't want," Bryan's rattling gasp punctuated the brief silence, "any money. Just let me go. I'll forget everything."

"I'm not worried about you telling a soul." The menace in the assailant's tone underscored his deadly

intent. "All I need to know is exactly where you hid it. If you tell me now, it will be a lot less painful."

"I can't—" Agony laced each word.

"What's that? A phone?" the man screamed.

The sounds of a struggle then a gunshot blasted her eardrum. Curses roared through the connection.

Fear paralyzed Annie in the middle of her kitchen. Was Bryan shot? Dead?

The voice on the phone returned. "Who's this? Who are you?"

The assailant's voice so clear on the phone panicked her. She slammed it down onto its cradle as though that action could sever the memories from her mind. But nothing would. Had she heard her daughter's father being killed? What information did Bryan have? Did that man know her name? Question after question bombarded her from all sides, but inertia held her still.

The ringing of the phone jarred her out of her trance. Her gaze zoomed in on the lighted panel on the receiver and saw the call was from Bryan's cell. The assailant had her home telephone number. He could discover where she lived. He knew what she'd heard.

"Mommy, what's wrong?"

Looking up at Jayden, Annie schooled her features into what she hoped was a calm expression while her stomach reeled. "You know, I've been thinking, honey, we need to take a vacation. It's time for us to have an adventure. Let's see how fast you can pack." Although she tried to make it sound like a game, her voice quavered, and Annie curled her trembling hands until her fingernails dug into her palms.

At the door, her daughter paused, cocking her head. "When will we be coming back?"

The question hung in the air, and Annie wondered if they'd ever be able to come back at all.

* * * * *

Follow Annie and Jayden as they flee to Christmas, Oklahoma, and hide from a killer—with a little help from a small-town police officer.

*Look for CHRISTMAS PERIL
by Margaret Daley and Debby Giusti,
available December 2009
from Love Inspired® Suspense.*

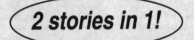

REQUEST YOUR FREE BOOKS!

2 FREE INSPIRATIONAL NOVELS
PLUS 2
FREE
MYSTERY GIFTS

YES! Please send me 2 FREE Love Inspired® novels and my 2 FREE mystery gifts (gifts are worth about $10). After receiving them, if I don't wish to receive any more books, I can return the shipping statement marked "cancel". If I don't cancel, I will receive 4 brand-new novels every month and be billed just $4.24 per book in the U.S. or $4.74 per book in Canada. That's a savings of over 20% off the cover price. It's quite a bargain! Shipping and handling is just 50¢ per book.* I understand that accepting the 2 free books and gifts places me under no obligation to buy anything. I can always return a shipment and cancel at any time. Even if I never buy another book, the two free books and gifts are mine to keep forever.

113 IDN EYK2 313 IDN EYLE

Name	(PLEASE PRINT)	
Address		Apt. #
City	State/Prov.	Zip/Postal Code

Signature (if under 18, a parent or guardian must sign)

Mail to Steeple Hill Reader Service:

IN U.S.A.: P.O. Box 1867, Buffalo, NY 14240-1867
IN CANADA: P.O. Box 609, Fort Erie, Ontario L2A 5X3

Not valid to current subscribers of Love Inspired books.

Want to try two free books from another series?
Call 1-800-873-8635 or visit www.morefreebooks.com

* Terms and prices subject to change without notice. Prices do not include applicable taxes. Sales tax applicable in N.Y. Canadian residents will be charged applicable provincial taxes and GST. Offer not valid in Quebec. This offer is limited to one order per household. All orders subject to approval. Credit or debit balances in a customer's account(s) may be offset by any other outstanding balance owed by or to the customer. Please allow 4 to 6 weeks for delivery. Offer available while quantities last.

Your Privacy: Steeple Hill Books is committed to protecting your privacy. Our Privacy Policy is available online at www.SteepleHill.com or upon request from the Reader Service. From time to time we make our lists of customers available to reputable third parties who may have a product or service of interest to you. If you would prefer we not share your name and address, please check here. ☐

LIREG09

Love Inspired®

HEARTWARMING INSPIRATIONAL ROMANCE

Get more of the heartwarming
inspirational romance stories that
you love and cherish, beginning
in July with SIX NEW titles,
available every month from
the Love Inspired® line.

Also look for our other
Love Inspired® genres, including:

Love Inspired® Suspense:
Enjoy four contemporary tales of intrigue
and romance every month.

Love Inspired® Historical:
Travel to a different time with two powerful
and engaging stories of romance, adventure
and faith every month.

Steeple
Hill®

LIINCREASE2

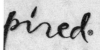

TITLES AVAILABLE NEXT MONTH
Available November 24, 2009

THE SOLDIER'S HOLIDAY VOW by Jillian Hart
The Granger Family Ranch

Trapped in a mine shaft with a little girl, September Stevens prays for help. And then she is rescued by handsome army ranger Mark Hawkins. Can his Christmas vow offer her the love of a lifetime?

JINGLE BELL BABIES by Kathryn Springer
After the Storm

When Nurse Lori Martin hears that Jesse Logan is looking for a nanny for his triplet daughters, she can't help but offer her services. Lori soon discovers that all she wants for Christmas is a trio of giggling babies—and their handsome father.

LONE STAR BLESSINGS by Bonnie K. Winn
Rosewood, Texas

Widowed sheriff Tucker Grey needs an instruction manual to raise his preteen daughter. Until Sunday school teacher Kate Lambert steps in. But can she teach the lawman to open his heart?

HIS CHRISTMAS BRIDE by Dana Corbit
Wedding Bell Blessings

The only gift Dylan Warren used to want was Jenna Scott's love. But his former childhood best friend broke his heart. Now, their matchmaking mothers insist the two families celebrate the holiday together. Will wedding bells join the jingle bells?

JENNA'S COWBOY HERO by Brenda Minton

Jenna Cameron has got a plan: raising her twin boys, running her ranch—and *not* falling in love. But brand-new neighbor Adam McKenzie has some plans of his own, which include building a summer camp—and a permanent place in Jenna's heart.

A WEDDING IN WYOMING by Deb Kastner

Jenn Washington has found a way to take the focus off her nonexistent love life. Her make-believe boyfriend "Johnny" should do the trick, until real cowboy Johnny Barnes shows up at the front door!

LICNMBPA1109